MIDNIGHT SERENADE

VEIL OF SHADOWS

BOOK TEN

M. R. PRITCHARD

About Midnight Serenade

Trapped between Heaven and Hell, Jed faces his demons while Shay's fate hangs in the balance.

Jed finds himself ensnared in a perilous web of darkness and despair as he confronts his inner demons. Shay's fate teeters on the edge of oblivion, her very existence hanging in the balance.

Driven by a thirst for vengeance, Alastor searches for a means to infiltrate the castle and unleash his wrath upon those who have wronged him. But his path is fraught with danger, and the shadows of betrayal lurk around every corner.

As if the looming threat of Alastor's revenge weren't enough, Nero's transformation into a monstrous entity sends shockwaves through the kingdom, casting a pall of fear and uncertainty over all who dwell within its walls. Outside the castle a malevolent presence lurks, waiting to unleash its fury upon any who dare to cross its path.

In this dark and twisted tale of betrayal, redemption, and the struggle for survival, Jed and Shay must navigate a treacherous landscape where the line between friend and foe blurs and the consequences of their choices echo through the halls of Hell itself. Will they find the strength to overcome the darkness that threatens to consume them, or will they be lost to its unforgiving embrace?

ONE

ALASTOR HEARD an echo that sounded more like the crunching of bones than the breaking of sticks underfoot. He shifted on his haunches and watched the Hellions survey the perimeter of the castle grounds.

Alastor gripped the basilisk tooth knife in his fist and turned only to find... nothing. There was nothing there, but the hairs rising on the back of his neck told him otherwise. Alastor felt something wasn't right as he began backing away. He needed a better plan than barreling in, especially because he heard someone walking nearby. Alastor shifted to get a good look at them; a Hellion. He was clearly young and must have pushed through the ranks to make guard duty. Alastor would use this weakness; the Queen's Commander unknowingly gifted the element of surprise since the recruit wouldn't have expected a Demon like Alastor to be hiding in the forest, searching for a way in.

Alastor waited until the Hellion got closer, and closer, and closer.

The Hellion was barely past puberty. Too bad. Alastor had to take this moment. He stood quickly and shoved the basilisk knife into the soft flesh under the Hellion's jaw. The Hellion never made a sound; he simply died in the forest.

Alastor made quick work of getting the Hellion's uniform off, then he stripped and put on. He took the blade knowing it wouldn't work for him; it was common knowledge that a Hellion's blade was enchanted to only cut for its owner. He had to look the part.

Alastor shivered. His bloodlines didn't run into Hellion territory and he knew nothing about honor and duty. Alastor was a different kind of Demon, his bloodline went to the root. Alastor could never join the Hellion ranks, but he could pretend. He could pretend until he made his way into that castle, killed the half-breed Angel, and took what was his. *Shay*. Alastor would use her as he wished, then sell her, piece by piece, until he'd collected all the money and power that was lost when his skin trade was disrupted.

Two

Jed was used to warding doors so no one could enter his room. He wasn't used to the opposite side of the door being locked so he couldn't exit. He tried the handle again and pulled. It wouldn't budge.

Jed's fingertips tingled as he drew on magic to open the door. He tried unlocking spells, opening spells, and transparency spells, but nothing worked. He paced the suite until he finally stopped next to the bed. Shay was sleeping. She'd been sleeping for more than a day. It had been a rough night with her breaking her leg again. She'd lost a lot of blood. He was sure that she was beyond tired after everything.

Jed bent and touched her forehead, remembering that he'd kept her up longer than he should have that night. Jed couldn't help it. He'd almost lost her. Need built within him as he remembered how he'd bathed the blood off her body, then carried her to the bed and gave her a few good reasons to never sneak off in the night again. There wasn't an inch of her body that he hadn't explored with his mouth, his tongue, his fingers. Desire stirred. He wanted her again. Again and again. Forever.

Shay shifted, rolling onto her stomach and pulling her right leg up. She was naked. The scar along her thigh was all he could see.

Jed lowered himself to the floor and kneeled. He moved his hand over the mark. There was something different about it. He closed his eyes and tried to get a sense of what was going on with the scar. His fingers glowed as he inspected the edges of it. He'd healed her femur; repaired the bone, muscle, and blood vessels. Something wasn't quite right though. The healing magic took, but it was almost as though something was lingering under her skin. Dirt, or a shard of... something. Jed wasn't sure. He wasn't a healer by trade, he simply had magic to help the healing process. Maybe he should consult Teari? The only problem was, he couldn't leave the room.

The sun was rising. Maybe Chel had locked them in here because whatever had spooked Skeele was still lurking in the forests surrounding the castle. Locking them up was a bit overboard. Certainly, they'd be safe within the walls of the castle. They'd be warm at least–winter chill was worsening.

Jed glanced at Shay's face. Chel probably didn't trust Shay to follow directions. Nero was still on the premises, roaming. He'd stood under the window and neighed sadly, calling for Shay. It was strange that the horse knew exactly which window was hers.

Shay sighed in her sleep. The sheet fell, revealing her bare shoulder. Her hair was longer--down the middle of her back. It had grown from one of the many healing spells he'd used.

Jed rubbed his face. He had plenty of questions, but right now no one wanted anything from either of them. He stripped off his clothes and crawled into bed next to Shay. She didn't protest as he dragged her body close to his and wrapped himself around her.

He could stay like this forever with her. Warm, safe, trapped. He'd let his guard down. It was easy, not looking over a shoulder and expecting danger every moment.

Jed pulled Shay's hair aside, revealing her neck. He watched her pulse, inspected her healed skin from the Hellion bite. He pressed his lips there, then across her neck to the sensitive skin behind her ear.

Shay nudged him with her hips. It was barely a movement, but he felt it and took it as an invitation. His free hand drifted down her body, lazily toying with her skin, her breasts, the plane of her stomach, edge of her ribs, the swell of her hips. Shay moaned and pressed against him. He parted her legs and nudged inside of her. He kissed her neck, her shoulder, and when his hand pressed against her lower belly, edging him deeper, her hand wrapped around his wrist and they fell away together.

THREE

NERO NIBBLED at the sweet grass that grew along the tree line. A crew was fixing the damaged barn but Nero had no desire to be contained by four walls ever again. He considered drinking from the nearby ponds but the Hellion who'd called him chum left out buckets of water. Nero was glad he wouldn't have to risk a stomach ache.

Nero stood near the Hellion training grounds, watching them train in combat. Something was wrong with Shay. Nero could sense her fatigue. After that night in the barn, the tether connecting them felt stronger, tighter. He wasn't sure why.

When she didn't come to the window, he'd felt disparaged. All he wanted was to see her and make sure she was okay. He'd apologize if he could. He never meant to hurt her. Never in his life would he do that intentionally. She was small and fragile, and he was so much bigger than he used to be. Still, Nero would watch over Shay. Nero would help her like she'd helped him when he was a foal.

He felt much stronger now that the basilisk had removed all the poison from his wound. There was barely an ache as it finished healing overnight.

The Hellion named Chel had threatened to make him leave, but there had been no official order. Nero liked the castle grounds. It was warmer than the forests and the mountains. He'd found a crack in an outcropping of rocks that leaked warm steam. Nero never wanted to return to that hovel. He'd do everything to stay here, close to Shay. This wasn't the Earthen plane. There were too many dangers.

"It's still out there," Klaus said to Tukka. "Whatever Skeele sensed is still here, somewhere."

Nero was listening and wandered closer.

"Keep up the reconnaissance." Tukka crossed his arms and frowned. "We're down three Hellions. We need to replace them."

"Call upon the families for more recruits. They'll be young." Klaus motioned to the recruits, and they switched sparring partners.

Nero nudged Klaus's shoulder, wishing he could speak and tell them he'd help.

"What do you want, beast?" Klaus smiled as he stroked Nero's nose. "You probably don't need to be pet like a puppy."

Nero huffed and nudged him again. He didn't mind the contact, it made him remember the days when everyone pet him. He'd received much less affection since Hell became his home.

"What about the family out there at the chapel?" Tukka motioned to the road. "Whatever's out there could be hunting them."

"Let's hope not." Klaus rubbed his white beard. "If anything happens to that baby, Meg will lose it."

Nero's ears twitched. He didn't realize there was a child so close. Since he had nothing to do, he decided he'd go investigate. Shay needed him but he could help protect the child as well. It was the least he could do for moving in uninvited.

Nero walked away from the Hellions and made his way across the yard. He left hoofprints on the rock path and overgrown grass. Nero avoided the stained dirt where the three Hellions had died. He didn't want to remember that night, what he'd done, or what he'd turned into.

Nero shook his head before glancing up at Shay's

window. It was still closed, the curtains pulled. He hoped she'd come out soon.

He passed the courtyard with the dead-looking tree in the center and headed for the main road that led to the graveyard. He'd seen it the night he ran here to find Shay.

Nero took his time, taking in his surroundings, searching for whatever threat was out here. His pace was lazy and slow but he made it to the graveyard faster than he expected.

There was a fence surrounding the chapel and Nero could hear the laughter of a young child. He remembered the joy of seeing children in Lame Deer and wandered closer.

The fence was tall but Nero could still see over it. He was sure he could leap over it if he needed to.

"Oh look, Thrush," a familiar voice said. "It's Nero."

He recognized Noah.

"Horsey," Noah said to the chubby baby in his arms. "Want to pet the horsey?"

"Are you sure that's a horse?" a woman's voice asked.

Nero tilted his head to see a woman with dark hair walking closer. Ah, Nightingale, the mother of the baby. He remembered now. Noah spoke of her when he'd visited Nero for the basilisk therapy.

"Big horsey," Noah said, bouncing the baby in his

arms. He stopped near the fence. "How'd you get that tall, Nero? Just a few days ago you were shorter."

Nero huffed and shook his head. He wasn't sure how tall he was, just that he could see over this fence and he was sure he'd never been able to do that before.

"Suppose you can't really tell me." Noah lifted baby Thrush and held him closer. "Horsey. Touch him."

A fat little hand reached out and touched the side of Nero's face. The baby laughed and babbled.

"Does he want a treat?" Nightingale asked, passing a carrot into Thrush's hand, helping him hold it up.

Nero took the carrot–easy and careful like Shay trained him–and chewed it, watching Thrush giggle as he crunched loudly.

Nightingale looked up as a shadow passed overhead. A Hellion was flying, scoping out the grounds. Nero wished he could speak and tell them that something dangerous was in the forest. He watched Nightingale closely and got the sense that whatever it was, should be afraid of her.

The wind was chilly, and baby Thrush was bundled up in a snowsuit. His cheeks were red.

Nightingale rubbed her arms and shivered. "We should get him inside," she said. "It's going to snow tonight."

Noah held Thrush close. "You stay warm tonight, Nero. Visit us again whenever you'd like."

Nero whinnied before turning and wandering toward the road.

As he walked, he heard Nightingale's voice mention *giant* and *Demon horse* and *dangerous*. But, the good thing about being a horse was he didn't have to give two shits about what people said about him.

Snowflakes were falling, leaving stark white dots against Nero's coat. He shook his head as they collected on his eyelashes.

A strange smell wafted from the forest. Nero paused and moved closer. Frozen leaves crunched under his hooves as he searched for the smell. It was familiar, something rotting. He wondered if this was what the Hellions were worried about. He searched and searched. Tree trunks scraped against his sides as he walked through the forest. Some trees bent or snapped off, too close together to accommodate his size.

Finally, he found it. A rotting corpse of a Demon under the leaves. A sense of pride filled Nero. He'd solved their problem and found the smell and the creature the Hellions were wary of. There was no danger after all.

Nero returned to the castle grounds and approached the first Hellion he came across.

He neighed and nodded his head. He walked back and forth, tugging on the Hellion's uniform with his teeth.

"Get away," the Hellion said, stepping back. "Shoo." He gripped his blade.

Nero gave up. This creature wasn't understanding that he had to show him something. He left and went in search of someone who might listen to him. Maybe that Hellion who'd called him chum, or their leader Skeele, or maybe he'd go back and get Noah. Who he really needed was Shay, she'd understand that he was trying to tell them something important.

Four

Then

CHEL LAY in the Hellion recruit barracks, hands behind his head, feet crossed, waiting for the bullshit to start. He'd been awake for hours, waiting for the Commander to come in shouting and dragging him and the rest of the Hellion recruits out of bed. His father had warned him it would be like this. His family was bred to be Hellions but something changed when Lucifer died and the new Queen took over. There was a shift in the edge that drove Hellions to violence. They held back, anticipated, contained their rage for only necessary times. They slept lighter and trained harder. New concepts had been taught like compassion and delayed reaction. In two days

Chel would be released on forty-eight hours of leave. He had nowhere else to go besides home.

Chel would never forget when he stepped through the threshold, the familiar sights and sounds of his childhood greeted him with a bittersweet embrace. The air was still heavy with grief, the weight of loss palpable in every corner, especially the kitchen where his mother spent most of her time.

Chel's mother hadn't spoken much during dinner, her eyes hollow with sorrow. She sat in silence, hands clasped tightly in her lap as if trying to hold on to the fragments of her shattered world. She'd been like this since Yelena went missing.

His father was a brooding figure in his favorite lounge chair, radiating an aura of simmering anger, his jaw clenched with unspoken fury. Chel remembered the same Demon from childhood. He hadn't changed a bit.

"Utter bullshit," his father slammed a fork down. "I didn't send my only son off to be a pussy in the ranks." He reached across the table and grabbed Chel by the collar of his uniform. "You listen to me, you smile and nod but deep down understand that mentality will not save a soul. You need to be quick, exact. You need to kill. That is a Hellion's duty."

"Yes, sir," Chel had nodded and stared into his father's red eyes until the moment of rage passed.

There it was. Sparrow, the Hellion Commander, had mentioned the rage that drove previous ages. They were going to be different, better. Sparrow's teaching and guidance was always inspiring, but Chel didn't tell his father that. He finished his dinner and came to the realization that this might be the last time he visited his parents.

Chel's mother stood and began clearing dishes. She left the dusty plate at the setting next to Chel. Yelena's seat. She'd never cleared the place setting after all these years. It was like she was expecting Yelena to come running back home and burst through the door for dinner. She never came, she would never come. Yelena had been gone for years; kidnapped and murdered by wrath-filled Demons.

Chel's gaze shifted to the empty space where Yelena once sat, a void that echoed with the haunting absence of her presence. The ache of her loss weighed heavily on his heart, a reminder of the fragility of life and the cruel whims of fate.

As the evening wore on, Chel found himself grappling with a revelation that gnawed at the core of his being. His father's violent outbursts and callous disregard for Yelena's death stirred a wellspring of conflicting emotions within him: a potent brew of anger, sadness, and a dawning realization that threatened to shatter his sense of identity.

In a moment of clarity, Chel realized that he could no longer ignore the toxic legacy of his father's behavior. He could not condone the cycle of violence and indifference that had plagued his family for far too long. He was not his father, and he refused to allow himself to become a reflection of the man who had brought so much pain and suffering into their lives.

"Do you have any news of Yelena's body being found?" Chel asked his father.

"Who cares?" his father shouted. "She's gone. Just another damned Demon woman, they make more every day."

"Yelena was more. Your wife is more. Do you not give a fuck about either of them?" Chel challenged the Demon. He spoke of the love and warmth that Yelena had brought into their lives; cozy evenings reading, dancing, picking flowers. The memories were a stark contrast to the darkness that his father's rage had wrought upon their family.

His father's anger boiled over and Chel stood his ground, refusing to back down. "I'm going to be better than you and if I ever have a wife or daughter I will love them more than you have ever loved anything."

"Get out of my fucking hovel with that mouth. You're nothing but a piece of shit. Hellions in my day didn't give a fuck about women or children. You were bred to serve the throne. Wait and see where this new ideology takes you all. You'll be dead in no time, and well deserved. Fuck off." Chel's father stormed off, disappearing to a room in the back of the hovel and slamming the door.

His mother hugged him. "You're a good Demon." There were tears in her eyes. "Yelena would be proud. I'm proud." She was taking off her apron and threw it aside. "I'll be leaving here now."

"I'll take you elsewhere. You can't stay here," Chel said.

She pulled a bag from under the sink. "I have only stayed this long for you, but I don't think you'll be back."

Chel shook his head. "I'll never see him again."

His mother nodded, wiping tears from her face. "There's a place I can go." She was shaking her head. "It's safe. Private."

"Good." Chel reached for the door. "Let's get you out of here."

His mother walked outside and Chel grabbed his gear and belongings. He closed the door to the hovel, taking one last glance at his family home. "Goodbye," he whispered.

Chel turned to face his mother. Walking closer, he

wrapped his arm around her narrow shoulders. In that moment, Chel realized that he was not defined by the sins of his father, not bound by the chains of past Hellions. He was a warrior, a protector, and above all a son who refused to let the darkness of his father's legacy extinguish the light of hope that burned within him.

They walked down a dirt path. The sounds of furniture breaking and angry shouting came from the hovel. As they moved on, Chel vowed to honor Yelena's memory by forging a new path; one guided by empathy, tenderness, and the unwavering belief that he could be the change that his family so desperately needed.

The reign of Lucifer was over, the darkness that had infiltrated every corner of Hell was slowly dispersing.

FIVE

Shay was still asleep. It had been too long–she'd been sleeping for days. He touched the scar on her thigh. It shined silvery and red. Healing magic lit his fingertips as he attempted to heal it further. Nothing happened.

Jed watched her face, relaxed, unknowing of his worry. He could have done it, erased her memories and sent her back to Montana. He could still do it. She'd been terribly injured twice now, and Jed was sure it wouldn't be the last time. This place was not for humans. The Earthen plane was rebuilding now that the Fast-Zombie War was over. She would be better off without him.

No. He closed his eyes to reset his thoughts. No. Jed promised her. Jed promised himself. He'd do better.

He touched her face, his fingertips still glowing. She slept but nuzzled his palm like a cat.

"Wake up, Shay-baby," Jed whispered. "You need to wake." He tucked blue hair behind her ear.

Nothing.

Jed stood, made his way to the door to their suite and tried to open it.

Nothing.

He scrubbed his head and tugged at his overgrown hair. He needed out of these rooms.

———

Then

Under the cloak of night, a moonless sky painted in inky darkness, Clara clutched Jed tightly to her chest as they fled through the twisting alleyways of the city.

"Don't look in its eyes," Clara whispered.

Jed was barely three. He was old enough to understand the fear in her voice.

"Don't, baby. Look at me."

Jed stopped looking over his mother's shoulder and buried his face in her neck, squeezing his eyes shut.

The cobblestone streets, worn and weathered, echoed with the urgency of Clara's footsteps as she navigated the labyrinth of buildings. Shadows danced on the walls like malevolent specters, a silent reminder of the pursuit.

"It's okay." Clara ran faster. Her footsteps echoed on the cobblestone road. It was dark outside and Jed could barely see a thing.

Jed knew it wasn't okay. He'd seen the monster lurking outside the diner window. His mother hadn't listened to him when he pointed and tried to tell her. He didn't know the exact words to say. But then, they couldn't stay at the diner all night, he knew that.

Clara's hand pressed on Jed's back to hold him in place. Jed's eyes were wide as he clung to her neck, his small fingers twisting in her shirt.

Something growled in the distance, reverberating through the night. Clara stole glances over her shoulders, glimpsing at the dark creature pursuing them. It had red eyes and scaled arms and lurked after them like some type of dog.

Clara turned a corner into a dimly lit alley. The moonlight broke through the clouds, painting fractured patterns on the cobblestones, revealing intricate carving and runes etched into the stones. Jed didn't know how to make the shapes, but he knew they were important.

The door to their apartment was close. Clara moved toward the doorstop wishing she'd taken the time to extend the runes to the door. It was only a few feet, but the Demon was too close. Clara hesitated as the demonic growls drew nearer, their presence palpable in the cool night air.

Clara set Jed on his feet and tucked him behind her. "Hold on to me," she told him. "Keep your eyes closed."

It growled, sounding like a dog or a tiger. Jed wasn't sure. He'd only gotten one good glimpse at it.

"Come on, you bastard," Clara called into the shadows.

Jed wanted to cry, but he was too scared. He could hear the Demons' nails clicking on the cobblestone as it paced.

Clara made a clicking noise, taunting the Demon. She reached in her skirt and pulled out a long hunting knife. With her free hand, she reached back and pressed Jed against her legs.

He squeezed his eyes shut, felt the thud of the creature against Clara's legs as it dove at her.

Clara chanted strange words and the Demon creature yelped like a kicked dog.

Jed opened his eyes. It had stopped attacking. There was blood on the cobblestone and his mother's hand was bloody.

"Inside! Now, baby," Clara rushed him to leave the rune circle. She unlocked the door with her clean hand and pushed him inside. "Stay here for me, baby." She looked him in his eyes. "I'll be back in just a few minutes. Okay?"

Jed nodded as she closed the door and locked it. He waited, sitting on the floor. He didn't know how to tell time, but it felt like he was waiting forever. His belly hurt and he was tired. He didn't like being locked in dark rooms. Jed wanted to shout and cry, wanted to scream for his mother to come back. But he knew that if he did that, the monsters would come. And he didn't want the monsters to come. He didn't want to cause his mother any more trouble.

Jed's eyes were nearly closed when the door opened again. His mother walked in, blood staining her skirts. "Just a moment, baby." She locked the door and walked past him, running the water in the sink, and scrubbing her hands.

He didn't know what she'd been doing, all he knew was that he never wanted to be locked in a dark room again.

SIX

Then

SHAY WASN'T WEARING anything especially revealing but tight jeans, cowboy boots, and a tank top turned nearly every head in the house when she opened the door to that dive bar. This was her last night of freedom–if she survived.

Shay looked over her shoulder one last time before the door closed. There were no strange noises outside, no gunshots, no squealing tires. The dive bar outside of Lame Deer wasn't too far from home but just far enough for her to feel a sense of freedom. Daddy and Momma would be pissed once they found out she'd snuck out her bedroom window and climbed down the porch supports. Hopefully they wouldn't find out. She was angry with them but didn't want to completely disappoint them. What did it matter anyway? Her life would never be what she wanted it to be.

She'd never been to a place like this, but she'd been around rowdy cowboys most of her life. It wasn't much different than the energy of the bull rider shows she'd been too. The only difference was she didn't have Daddy on her hip, nor Momma waiting in the stands. And she was grown, looking to feel something more than disappointment.

Shay kept her chin up and ignored the fluttering in her heart as she walked to the bartender.

"What'll you have, little lady?" the bartender asked.

"Rum and coke." Shay didn't normally drink, but it was the only thing she could think of. It rolled off her tongue nicely, and she figured she could like asking for something other than a fruity drink or plain beer.

She sipped at her drink and watched the bull riders on the television screen. Her eyes drifted down to the zombie warnings streaming across the bottom of the screen. California was overrun and so was the East Coast. Shay was grateful for living in the Midwest. The hell that had broken loose was trickling in.

Her eyes flicked around the room as she sipped at her

drink. She sagged against the high-back of her barstool and crossed her legs.

It wasn't long before she was interrupted.

"What's your name, Cowgirl?" a handsome guy asked.

"Shay." She'd planned on lying about her name but when it came down to it, she couldn't. Shay had never been a good liar, she'd much rather tell the truth and move on.

"That's a nice name for a pretty girl." He touched her hair.

Craving the attention, Shay leaned toward his hand and looked down. She wasn't sure what to do exactly, she'd never done this kind of thing before.

"What are you having to drink?" the cowboy asked.

The bartender made a face of trepidation as he poured another rum and coke.

"What's your name?" Shay asked the cowboy. She liked his dark eyes and wide smile, the dimple in his cheek. He talked with a western accent that was hard to place.

"Clyburn." He sipped at his beer.

Shay and Clyburn talked about horses and ranches.

"Are you here alone?" he finally asked.

The bartender's eyes flicked to Shay.

She could tell he was wary of the cowboy, but Shay had come here with a purpose. One last night of fun.

She nodded and threw back the rest of her rum and coke. She motioned for another drink and took money out of her pocket to pay for it.

"No, sweety, I got it." Clyburn touched her hand.

Shay was thinking about the feeling of his fingertips, how they'd feel touching the rest of her skin. She glanced up at him and his pupils widened.

Shay took another sip of her fresh rum and coke, feeling tipsy when someone turned up the jukebox. Southern rock was playing. A few couples had shown up during the night and were dancing.

Clyburn noticed her watching. "Come on." He took her hand and dragged her to the dance floor. Shay had never been dancing with a man before. Suddenly she fully realized how sheltered her life was. No boyfriends, no freedom, nothing–especially now that the apocalypse had arrived. Shay couldn't go on knowing she'd never lived fully; she could die at any moment. A need to experience it all bloomed in her chest. Shay's body moved in rhythm with Clyburn and the music. He touched her hip and she touched his shoulder. His thumb slid under the hem of her shirt, stroking the soft skin of her stomach.

Shay's fingertips stretched up the side of his neck and into his dark hair.

Clyburn pulled her close.

He smelled like liquor and tobacco. Like bales of hay and manly musk.

She toyed with the button of his shirt with her free hand. He tugged her close until their bodies were touching. Her hips gyrated with the music. His thigh slid between hers and pressed against her core. Sweat slid down Shay's back as a hunger grew within her belly.

Clyburn touched her and held her tight and she let him, never having known a man's touch like this before. She liked it. He was strong. His hands felt good. They moved together during the brief silence between songs.

They danced like this until the bar started to empty out and the jukebox music came to an abrupt stop.

"Last call," the bartender shouted.

The spell that had struck Shay broke. She blinked and looked up at Clyburn. His pupils were wide, his lips parted. Shay wanted to kiss him, so... she did.

He tasted like liquor. Fresh and warm. Shay pressed her body to his, closer. She wanted to be closer.

Clyburn pulled away, gripping her hips. "Christ, girl," he swore.

"I don't want to go home." Shay's fingers twisted in his shirt.

He nodded, leading them back to their drinks.

Shay threw back the last of her rum and coke. Clyburn paid the tab then led her out the door.

"I'm parked around back." He gripped her wrist.

Shay felt light, energized. She'd never been this drunk before but all she could think was how she *wasn't* thinking, finally. For once in her life.

Vehicles were leaving as Clyburn led her to a big truck parked in the shadows.

"I don't have a place nearby," Clyburn warned as he pressed her back against the truck and kissed her.

"I don't care," Shay said. She reached for his shirt, working the buttons until she could press her palms against his hard chest.

Clyburn's hands were under her shirt, rubbing and kneading.

Shay felt like she was on fire. Like she was invincible. Like she could live forever.

Clyburn hesitated.

Shay pulled away and noticed the parking lot was empty. There was nothing but darkness and empty cow pasture behind them.

"Here," Shay whispered. "I don't care."

Clyburn pulled away from her, opened the truck, and pulled out a thick blanket. He laid it out in the truck bed then jumped down. His hands returned to her body, his lips to hers. They kissed, and he pulled her against him until they were at the tailgate. Clyburn lifted her. Shay took off her top and he followed.

She traced the ridges of his body, illuminated by moonlight, and reveled in his strength as he jumped into the truck bed and lifted her, bringing her to the blanket.

He was gentle. His mouth licked and bit her skin. He folded her jeans after dragging them down her legs. When he stretched his body over hers, Shay shivered feeling the bulge against her leg.

Clyburn was slow. Too slow. He paid too much attention. It made her sick. This wasn't what Shay wanted. She wanted something quick and dirty, something hard and fast. She wasn't looking for marriage, just a one night stand. Clyburn was turning this into something else. Shay's stomach lurched at the wrongness of it all. She sat up, shoving him off.

"You okay?" Clyburn asked, surprised.

Shay scrambled off the truck and puked into the grass at the edge of the parking lot.

"It's okay." Clyburn was close, holding her hair as the drinks from the bar forced their way out.

Shay heaved until there was nothing left. She sagged against the truck.

Clyburn started rubbing her back, then her hips.

"I'm not done," he whispered as he forced her to bend over and took her from behind.

The tailgate of the truck bit into her stomach. This was what Shay wanted. Something disgusting and heartbreaking. Something dirty and erasable.

He finally stopped and pulled out.

"Christ," he muttered. "There's blood." His voice shifted. "I'm sorry."

"It's fine." Shay reached for her clothes and got dressed faster than a fox in a hen house.

"Let me care for you–"

"No." Shay stopped him. "I didn't come here for that."

"What did you come for, little lady?" Clyburn was standing stark naked in the moonlight. He was a spectacle, a nearly perfect man; muscled and tall, dark hair and eyes.

"Forget this ever happened." Shay ran to her car. She was rapidly sobering up. Ignoring the ache between her thighs, she unlocked the driver door.

Clyburn caught up with her, grabbed her arm and turned her. "I don't understand."

"Ain't nothing for you to understand, cowboy." Shay searched his eyes, hoping he'd understand that she wanted nothing else to do with the man.

She left him with his jaw clenching in the dark parking lot.

Shay went home. She climbed the porch railing and opened her bedroom window. She showered the blood off her thighs and hid her dirty clothes.

The next morning, Shay got up and started breakfast like nothing had ever happened. She'd slept three hours.

"You feeling okay, hun?" Momma asked.

"Fine." Shay rubbed her face. "Just didn't sleep good."

"I heard you in the shower. Do you want some tea?"

Shay shook her head and continued cracking eggs into her bowl until she heard heavy, booted footsteps on the porch, Daddy's voice, and someone else's.

"We got a new ranch hand this morning. Lord knows we could use him," Momma said, wiping her hands on a towel. "Let's say hello."

Shay nodded and followed Momma to the screen door. She heard Daddy's voice as he introduced them. Shay looked up as the door closed and her eyes met familiar dark ones.

Clyburn.

Breath caught in her throat. There was a pain behind her ribs. No.

"Nice to meet ya, Shay." Clyburn held out a hand.

Shay didn't want her parents to know what she'd

done the night before. She couldn't let them know. Shay shook the familiar hand that was reaching for her. "Nice to meet you, cowboy."

Clyburn smiled. Shay's face was still as her lungs begged for air. She was sure she'd never drag another breath through them again. What in the hell was he doing here?

Daddy started talking about cattle and horses and led Clyburn off the porch. Momma opened the screen door. Wood creaked under Shay's feet as she tried to move.

It wasn't even worth what she'd gone through. Those few minutes with a handsome cowboy in a dive bar parking lot were definitely not worth losing everything. She knew she was going to lose everything. The premonition was overwhelming. A sickening emptiness filled her gut. Shay hated herself more than she hated anything on this planet.

As he walked toward the barn with Nicholas, Clyburn glanced back at her and winked.

———

Now

SHAY WOKE UP SCREAMING.

Jed heard her from the other room and ran in to find her staring blankly at the ceiling. He grabbed her shoulders and shook her until life re-entered her eyes. "Shay-baby, come back."

She focused on Jed's face before whimpering and scrambling onto his lap, her arms and legs gripping him tight.

It took him a moment to wrap his arms around her and rub her back. "It's okay," he murmured over and over again. "You're safe."

He rocked her, thinking about the speck of something that was locked under the scar on her thigh, wondering if maybe that had something to do with her screaming. Maybe it had something to do with the locked door and the sense of danger. He wasn't sure.

Shay's sobs finally ceased and she pressed her forehead against his collarbone. "Something bad happened," she said.

"Yeah." Jed stopped rubbing her back.

"I feel okay."

"You're looking much better than you were the other night."

"Tell me."

Jed took in a deep breath. "There were three Hellion recruits–"

"And Nero."

"Yes, and Nero."

"Is Nero okay?" Shay whispered.

"Nero is good."

There was a moment of silence as Shay plucked at Jed's shirt before she said, "Tell me more."

"The Hellions are dead. You broke your leg... again. It's mostly healed."

Shay's hand brushed over her thigh, feeling the scarred ridge on her skin. "It feels okay."

"Whatever Skeele sensed is still out there. We've been locked in our suite for a few days."

Shay sat up straight and leaned back. "Days?"

Jed searched her eyes, brushing her hair away from her face and cupping her jaw with both hands. "You're really feeling okay? What were you dreaming about?"

Shay's mouth parted, and she licked her bottom lip with the tip of her tongue. "Clyburn."

Jed scowled. "He's dead."

Shay nodded. "I remember. Nero killed him."

Jed wished it had been him. But his weakness was that he didn't know how to transverse realms during that time. He was thankful for Nero and what the horse had done when rescuing Shay. Even if it meant he'd changed into something else.

"The barn was destroyed," Jed continued, his thumb

rubbing her skin. "Workers have been fixing it little by little."

"Where has Nero been sleeping?" Shay asked.

"Where ever he wants." Jed motioned to the balcony window. "Sometimes he shows up there."

"That's good. I don't know what I'd do if I couldn't see him."

Jed released Shay's jaw and his hands slid down her neck to her shoulders and he rubbed her arms. "Are you hungry? You have eaten nothing in days."

Shay nodded and moved to crawl off his lap.

Jed stopped her by gripping her thighs. "Promise me you will never go outside alone again."

"That's ridiculous," Shay scoffed. "I can't promise that. I already promised I wouldn't go outside while you're sleeping."

"So you did remember something from the other night." Jed smirked.

SEVEN

ALASTOR COULD HANDLE THE WEAPONS; it was
the form of hand-to-hand combat that got him in trouble, got him noticed. The Hellion Commander, Skeele,
was watching him from the sidelines. He'd become
accustomed to his new name of Dalk and answered
when Skeele called him to the sidelines.

"Where did you learn to fight like that?" Skeele
asked.

Alastor didn't look directly at him when he replied,
"The hovels in the mountains."

"Hm." Skeele rubbed his face. "You're going to need
to work harder. An Angel would defeat you in a heartbeat with moves like those." Skeele paused, sniffed the
air, and glanced toward the forest.

"Yes, Sir," Alastor noted.

He went back to his sparring partner and wound up on his ass more than a handful of times. Alastor had underestimated Hellion recruit training. He'd lasted for decades with his skin trade but there were weapons and extra hands involved to help with fighting. He'd grown lax in his strength. Alastor promised to work harder. He'd need the strength to get Shay out of the castle.

Alastor had been there nearly a week and learned the daily agenda. Training, lunch, training, rounding on the royal grounds and nearby graveyard and a few other locations he'd not been privy to. Then more training. Alastor didn't care, he only needed to find where Shay was.

"Hey, Dalk." A Hellion recruit with a stubby nose nodded to him. "You look different than last time I saw you."

Alastor blinked. "Must be this slop." He scooped up a spoonful of gruel and dripped it back into the bowl.

The Hellion laughed and the conversation turned into razzing the terrible meals they got during the week.

"Can't wait for Sunday dinner." The Hellion licked his lips. "Don't know why they only give us the good food once a week."

Alastor ate and considered his next steps. He was fitting in more and more each day. He didn't get too close to the castle and he noticed there was a giant black horse wandering freely. There was something familiar about the creature.

Sunday dinner was a spectacle. It reminded Alastor of the Thanksgiving dinners on the Earthen plane. There were piles of food. A roasted pig, baked turkey, hamburgers, and hot dogs. Fresh vegetables and fruits. Beers and wine. Alastor waited in line to fill his plate and listened to the surrounding conversations.

"Don't know why they don't feed us like this all week."

"Cause you'd be fat."

"My gut would pop from all the beer."

"We'd be slow."

"Shut up."

"Hey, there's pie!"

Alastor ate more than he had in years. As he sipped at the beer, he watched the Hellion recruits around him go back for seconds and thirds. There was a limit of three servings on the alcohol. That was probably an excellent decision, Alastor thought. A barracks full of drunk Hellion recruits would be messy. He sidled up to the drunkest of the Hellion recruits to get some information out of him.

They clinked beer mugs. Alastor sat.

"I heard a rumor that a human was being kept nearby."

The drunk Hellion muttered something about "not in Lucifers day."

"Tragic what Hell has become with a woman on the throne." Alastor sipped at his beer. "Why a human though? Never had one in Hell before. Or at least never had one roaming around freely like a pet." He added a lewd laugh.

"Definitely should be kept in the dungeons and used for other things." The drunk Hellions lips became looser with each word. "She walks around here freely, sometimes with that crossbreed freak."

"I haven't seen them."

"Will do you good to ignore them. Last week they got three of us killed."

"I missed it."

"They got her blood. Got the blood lust and went hunting her. Commander made a spectacle out of it. Snapped their necks and left their bodies for all of us to see."

"Shit." Alastor sipped at his beer. "And yet so many recruits have stayed."

"Not one left," the Hellion recruit slurred.

"Why?"

"We are bred to serve, not think."

"Wouldn't take much to end a human."

"Get yourself on dungeon guard duty and you'll be

halfway there." He pointed toward the castle in the distance. "The horse goes to her window at night. Seen it with my own eyes." He poked two fingers toward his eyes. Beer dribbled down his chin.

"What floor is she on?" Alastor asked.

"Watch the horse." The Hellion recruit suddenly fell over, spilling his beer and snoring on the bench.

Alastor walked away from the drunk Hellion and made his way to the window. There were too many tables and bodies and noise. He veered toward the door, taking his drink with him.

There were shadows below an oak tree outside the Hellion recruit lounge. Alastor sat with his back against the trunk and watched the castle in the distance. The sun had set in Hellsky and the ochre moonglow illuminated the expanse of grass between the training grounds and the castle. It didn't take long for the large black horse to wander by without a care in the world. It stopped to nibble on grass and drink out of a bucket before meandering toward the castle.

Alastor sipped at his beer. That wasn't just a horse, he could tell. There was something wrong with it.

The horse stopped under a row of windows and whinnied, looking up.

Alastor watched the windows for movement. Then, curtains fluttered and a pale face looked out.

There she was.

Hell had changed Shay. She still had the blowtorch blue hair, but she looked paler than when he'd last seen her on the Earthen plane. He remembered the warmth of her skin, the shine in her eyes. She'd had more life than any of the women they'd captured for the skin trades. It was all the strength he contained to leave her alone in that cabin with a bowl of spaghetti, freshly showered. He should have touched her more then. Branded her. Taken her. Never let her leave. Chained her up and kept her for eternity.

Alastor drained his beer and stood. He knew where her window was. He knew she was weakened. Finding her room once he was inside the castle and getting her out would be a cake walk.

EIGHT

SHAY STOOD in a dimly lit cavern, shadows dancing ominously as Chel watched her with eyes like burning coals.

A few days had passed, and Shay had energy to train again. Actually, since leaving the suite her energy levels had increased by leaps and bounds. She felt as though she'd drank a pot of coffee and was ready to run some laps.

The air crackled with anticipation as Chel prepared for their training session.

"Where are the Hellion recruits?" Shay asked warily.

Chel stood to his full height. "They're elsewhere. They won't harm you."

Shay shivered. "Okay." Shay couldn't stop thinking about that night. She needed more time to process the memories. It was strange; everything coming back to her full force, the dreams of Clyburn. It was all too much right now.

"Maybe we should wait until next week," Chel suggested.

"No." Shay shook her head. "No more waiting. I needed fresh air. Been locked up in that room for too long. I feel good."

Jed was lingering nearby, watching them.

"It was for your safety." Chel passed Shay a wooden sword to practice with.

"The threat is gone now?" Shay asked.

"I wouldn't say that. Threats are never absent."

"You're a ray of sunshine, Chel." Shay bent her knees, wincing when pain sliced through her thigh.

"You're not ready."

"I'm ready. Let's just get this over with. Please." Shay gripped the wooden sword and swung it.

Chel jumped back. "Dang, woman."

It went on for another hour, Chel showing Shay how to wield a sword, then a hunting knife. He showed her where to hit an enemy. The throat, the solar plexus, the crotch.

"Listen carefully, Shay," Chel's voice resonated with a gravelly timbre, dripping with the weight of centuries of experience. "In the realm of darkness, survival hinges on mastery of the blade and the art of deception."

With a swift motion, Chel drew forth a wickedly curved blade, its surface glinting malevolently in the dim light of the cave. He tossed it to Shay, who caught it with a determined grip.

Chel's brows rose in surprise. "Good catch."

"Caught plenty of flying shit on the ranch back home," Shay said with a smile. "You should see me with a rope."

"The blade is an extension of your will," Chel instructed, his eyes burning with intensity. "Feel its weight, its balance. Let it become a part of you."

Shay nodded, her muscles tensing with anticipation as she poised herself for the onslaught of Chel's teachings. She'd done plenty of physical activity on the ranch with shooting and horse riding. Her father had taught her how to shoot a bow and wield a knife. The sword was just another tool, another extension of her body. She was simply facing different animals.

"Attack me," Chel commanded, his stance shifting into a defensive position, his eyes gleaming with anticipation.

Without hesitation Shay lunged forward, her movements fluid and graceful as she unleashed as series of strikes. But Chel, with the agility of a serpent, evaded each blow with uncanny precision, his movements a blur of darkness.

"Predictable," Chel's voice echoed with disdain as he countered Shay's attacks with lightning-fast strikes of his own, forcing her to retreat.

Gritting her teeth, Shay pressed on, her determination fueling her every move. She focused on Chel's movements, seeing an opening.

As the duel raged on, Shay's instincts sharpened, her movements becoming more fluid, more instinctual. With each exchange she learned, adapting her tactics to anticipate Chel's elusive maneuvers.

Jed watched quietly on the sidelines.

In a sudden burst of speed, Shay closed the distance between them, her blade flashing in the dim light as she launched a relentless assault. Chel staggered backward, a look of surprise flickering across his Hellion visage.

With a triumphant smirk, Shay pressed on, her strikes raining down upon Chel with unbridled ferocity. In a flurry of motion, she delivered a blow that sent him stumbling backward. Shay's chest heaved with exertion, her leg burned, her eyes blazed with newfound determination. She was more than just a human woman; she was a warrior, forged in the fires of darkness, ready to face whatever challenges lay ahead.

"Bring your head back down out of the clouds, Shay," Chel warned.

Shay blinked and focused on him.

"This was one session. We are far from done." Chel collected the swords and sheathed them. "If you stay in the realm of Hell, you need to keep training."

"Are you going to send me back to the Earthen plane?" she asked.

"No," Jed stepped forward. "He can't tell us to do anything."

Chel made a face. "I can tell you that you're both under curfew. Skeele wants you in your suite at sunset." Chel looked down at Shay. "It's for her safety."

NINE

Shay felt hot. It came on suddenly. She glanced at the roast beef on her plate and wondered if the food was bad. No. Not the food. She tried to take another bite but when the juices hit her tongue she gagged.

Shay moved her napkin to her mouth and spit out the meat so no one could see what she was doing. She folded the napkin and set it next to her plate.

Jed was watching her from across the table. He sipped at a glass of wine, toying with his fork, moving around perfectly seasoned asparagus. His eyes looked away for a second before landing on her face again.

"Okay?" he mouthed, concerned.

Shay shook her head. She wasn't okay. She was ready to blow chunks all over Meg's special family dinner night. The last time someone interrupted family dinner, Meg killed them. Shay's gaze roamed to Meg at the end of the table. She was eating and laughing at something Skeele said. Meg hadn't been in the killing mood since the Deacons released her from the Safe House. She'd actually calmed nearly eighty percent compared to how she was always on edge before. At least that was Shay's assessment of the Queen of Hell. Still, Shay didn't want to puke on the good China.

She pushed her chair back.

Chel turned to her, followed by the rest of the Hellions. Shay didn't want to make a scene, but it appeared it was too late.

"What's wrong?" Chel asked.

She couldn't shake the Hellion. He'd been up her ass since she arrived. They'd grown closer but she could tell by the way he looked at Jed, something wasn't right between the two of them.

"Nothing," Shay replied before standing and walking out of the room. "I'll be right back," she whispered to Meg with a wave.

The Queen of Hell nodded and Shay released a sigh of relief. Tonight wouldn't end with her as a bloodstain on the floor.

Shay pushed open the dining room door and leaned her cheek against the cool stone of the wall.

She heard footsteps, smelled something delectable. The feeling of wanting to vomit was replaced with her mouth watering. She turned and saw a small creature carrying a tray of meat. This time it was prepared for the Hellions. Bloody and raw, barely a sear. She wanted it, could barely control the urge to grab it off the tray.

"Can I have a piece of that?" Shay asked the creature.

It stopped for her and motioned in agreement.

Shay took a slice of the bloody meat and licked it. Amazing. Better than anything she'd ever eaten before. She shoved the slice of meat in her mouth. It was so good. She wanted more. She turned to get another piece but the creature was walking into the dining room. Through the open door, she saw Jed and Chel making their way toward her.

She turned and walked down the hallway as fast as she could. Shay felt better having eaten the nearly raw meat, but she knew that wasn't right. She'd never eaten raw meat before.

"Shay!" Jed called after her. "Wait up."

Crap. Shay started walking away from them.

Footsteps followed. Shay walked faster. "I'm just going to get some fresh air."

"No you're not," Chel warned. "It's past your curfew."

Her heart beat against her ribs. She needed out of

here. Shay needed some freedom, needed air and peace. She needed the ochre shine of Hellnight on her skin.

"Just a few minutes," Shay shouted over her shoulder.

The footsteps behind her turned heavy. The men were running.

Something like electricity zipped up her spine. Shay ran. She was close to the door. She could make it. Shay ran faster, arms out and ready to push the door open. She was close. So close.

She made it. She shoved the centuries-old wood and ran into the courtyard, heart thumping and throat aching with dryness.

Sharp pain shot up her leg. It came from her scar. Her leg felt strange, not right. It felt heavier, longer. She stumbled then tripped. Shay held her hands out to catch her as she fell but the courtyard ground was uneven. Her hands slid, torn up by rough rock. She cried out just before she hit her head and knocked herself unconscious.

———

Jed could barely believe his eyes as Shay's leg flickered. There was something wrong with it. It didn't look like the rest of her body. It was twisted and shaped strangely, but only for a moment before it went back to normal. Like a mirage, like something was messing with his vision.

Chel made a noise of irritation as he kneeled next to Shay and rolled her over. "Fucking woman." His eyes flashed red as he looked at Jed. "What's gotten into her?"

Jed healed Shay's hands first. He didn't want to risk her blood spilling on Meg's land again and risking the Hellions coming after her. He worked fast, watching her shallow breaths. His hands drifted to her jawbone, healing a scrape. Then to the sides of her head.

The urge was there, still. The urge to clear her mind of all this and send her away. The Fast-Zombie War was over. She'd be safe rebuilding on the Earthen plane. He swallowed against a dry throat. Jed could protect her from afar. He could linger nearby and let her live a life without all this darkness. Jed's fingertips tingled with magic.

"What the fuck are you doing?" Chel shoved at Jed's hands. "Don't dig your hole deeper."

Jed moved his hands lower, searching for injuries, and when he found none he lifted her. "Let's get her to the infirmary and send for Teari." He held her limp body close, wanting nothing more than to heal and protect her from whatever was going on inside her body.

Chel held the door open as they walked inside the castle. He paused, glancing across the dry grass as movement caught his eye. There was something shifting in the shadows. It stepped out, into the ochre moonlight.

Nero.

TEN

NERO FELT it all happening through the thread that connected him to Shay. He didn't know transforming into the Demon would affect her. He didn't know she'd crave blood and freedom like he did.

Nero shook the dark energy off his hide. The transformation was still new to him. His long black tail and mane were stiff as needles and sharp as razorblades. His veins were giant ropes of obsidian under his skin, twining and swirling like protective armor. He turned into something less.

He had been on the other side of the cemetery. There was something bad lingering over there. Something worse than him. Worse than the creature who'd invaded the royal grounds then went incognito. Nero had gone to investigate.

It was a Demon and it was too close to Thrush. Nero wouldn't risk danger coming that close to Nightingale and Thrush. He was sure Noah could handle himself, could probably protect his family but Nero wouldn't stand down. He'd sensed it and searched for it. No one else had come looking for the danger. It made Nero wonder how strong the Hellion's inherent sense of danger toward the Queen and her land was.

He'd searched Hellforest and found a creature that looked like a cloud. It undulated maniacally, surged toward him and tried to pass. He wouldn't let the creature hurt the little boy who'd pet his snout so curiously. He wouldn't let it get near Shay. Nero had no choice but to transform and defeat it. When it was dead and dropped to the ground like black mist, Nero ate it.

It tasted like licorice and blackberries. And while there were no bones, its cotton-candy texture crunched between his giant teeth and echoed throughout Hellforest.

Only afterwards did he feel the tug from Shay; her unease and nausea, her panic and fear as she ran.

Nero was running toward her, back to the castle. It didn't take him long in this form. When he saw her run into the courtyard from the shadows, he transformed to the Nero she knew. He didn't want to scare her. But then she fell. He watched from a distance, afraid that Chel would cast him out if he saw Nero changing and lingering. The Hellion was overprotective of Shay and the royal grounds. Not as bad as Skeele, but close.

Eleven

"Your leg is still bothering you?" Teari asked.

Shay was sitting on a bed in the infirmary. "It aches sometimes." She touched the stiff sheets.

"Jed is worried about it." Teari held her hands over the scar.

Shay was staring at the ceiling, ignoring the sharp pains that jolted up her leg every few minutes.

"Sometimes?" Teari asked.

"Yes," Shay lied. "Just every now and again." Shay sighed. She didn't want to be in the infirmary. She didn't understand why Teari wouldn't meet her somewhere else. This room was too white. Too pristine. Too cold. There was no smell to it. Shay supposed it was a hygienic measure, she didn't have to enjoy it.

"Were you bit by a Demon?" Teari asked.

Shay shook her head.

"Cut with a Demon blade?" Teari asked.

Shay shook her head again.

Teari made a face.

"What?" Shay asked.

"Jed was right. There's something trapped in this scar."

Shay wanted to tell her about eating the raw meat and enjoying it. She wanted to tell her about running away and her leg feeling changed. It sounded so stupid though. She was human, unlike the beings she was now surrounded with. Her body didn't have magic or the ability to transform. She was sick. That was all. Whatever sickness had infected her was driving her insane.

"Noah," Teari called.

A few minutes passed before Noah appeared in the room.

"Thank you for coming." Teari smiled.

"I'll take a break from searching the ends of Hell for Meg's snacks." He rubbed his face with both hands. "That woman is insufferable."

"Show some compassion," Teari said. "She's under a lot of stress. And she's with child."

Noah took a deep breath and rolled his eyes exaggeratedly. "What do you need?"

"A small Basilisk." Teari smiled.

Noah made a face and shuddered. "Of course." He disappeared.

Teari turned to Shay. "Poor guy doesn't like the creatures."

"Is this going to hurt?" Shay asked.

"No." Teari was watching Shay closely. "Jed said you looked sick at dinner last night. Tell me about that."

Remembering the foul taste of the cooked meat on her plate, Shay swallowed hard. The sensation hadn't hit her today but Shay was wary it would come back again.

"I'm just going to check your stomach and see what's going on." Teari's hands hovered over Shay's skin, from her leg to her hip, over her pelvis, to her stomach, ribcage. She stopped at Shay's center and closed her eyes.

"What do you think–" Shay was about to ask what was wrong but Noah opened the door, carrying a heavy basket. She saw two shadows in the hall outside the door.

Noah thumbed toward the door that was closing. "You got a line out there."

"Who?" Shay asked.

"It's Jed and Chel. They're concerned." Teari moved to the side so Noah could set the basket down near Shay's injured leg.

He opened the flip top and removed the small

Basilisk and held it steady, mouth pointed toward Shay's scar.

The Basilisk turned away. It thrashed and whipped its head, trying to escape and having no interest in the Demon venom that was trapped in Shay's scar. This went on for minutes until Noah's hands were thick with slime that dripped on the white floor.

Teari was talking to the creature, trying to encourage it. "You can do it. Right there."

"Maybe you should open it up," Noah suggested.

Shay and Teari looked to a nearby table with neatly arranged tools and surgical blades.

"Don't," Shay flinched. "I'm tired of cuts and wounds and magical healing. Maybe all this is unnecessary."

Shay covered her bare leg. "Get it out of here." She waved at the Basilisk. "Take it back. I don't want to try this." Shay was feeling sick again. The smell of the Basilisk slime made her stomach roil.

"You don't want it to heal you?" Teari asked.

"I don't want my leg cut open again." Shay rubbed the scar through the sheet.

"Even if it fixes you?" Teari asked.

Noah was wrestling the Basilisk to get it in the basket again. He stood, flipping his shaggy hair and wiping his hands on his pants. "Fine with me," he said. "I'd prefer not to have to fetch these blasted things every time someone gets a little Demon poison in them." He scoffed like it was the worst job in the world.

"I'm fine," Shay said. "It's just some lingering pain and a stomach bug. I don't understand why you are all so concerned."

Noah left the room with the Basilisk basket.

Shay threw the rough sheet off her body and got dressed. She didn't care if Teari saw her.

"You should stay here and rest," Teari offered. "I can give you something to help."

"No." Shay shook her head. "I'm going to sleep in my bed." Shay headed for the door. "Thanks for the help, Teari," she said over her shoulder.

Shay shoved the door open, hoping to hit the two men waiting on the other side.

Jed and Chel jumped back.

"Are you okay?" Jed asked.

"Fine." Shay walked past him and headed for the staircase.

The two men looked at each other, wondering if they should follow.

"I'm going to bed." Shay's heavy footsteps echoed as she stomped up the winding staircase.

Shay opened the door to the suite she shared with Jed. The familiar runes and markings were everywhere.

Suddenly, it all looked so chaotic. It made her anxious. She wanted just a normal room with normal walls and floors and window casings. Shay didn't want to see that Jed feared her weak humanity at every turn. She was tired of it.

Shay went to the closet and changed her clothes. She put on a dark pair of jeans, a button-down flannel that was soft and worn, then her boots. She grabbed a hunting knife and her pistol.

Shay walked to the balcony, threw open the doors and leaned against the railing. Women had a habit of throwing themselves off the railings here. Someone should probably do something about that.

Nero was waiting below. The drop wasn't far at all. Shay's gaze went to the exterior wall. There were vines and jutting rocks. She might break her neck but she'd climbed worse in Montana. Once she'd scaled a rock wall to the valley below and tied Nicholas's rope around a calf that had fallen. That was at least twice as tall as the distance below the balcony.

Shay threw her leg over the railing and climbed down.

TWELVE

TEARI STOOD in the infirmary with Jed and Chel.

"I'm going to have to do some research." Teari tapped a finger on her chin, thinking. "Something is off and I'm not sure what it is."

"She's different," Jed said. "Shay was training with Chel and almost sliced him through. She's stronger."

"Strength isn't a bad thing." Teari was searching Jed's face. "There's more?"

Jed tried not to think about how beautiful Teari was, how white her wings were, how he wanted to tell her everything. He assumed that was part of being a royal healer. She was easy to talk to, gave him diarrhea of the mouth. Or maybe it was him, finally spending time with an Angel that didn't include a death match. He wanted it to go on forever.

"After she was injured again, it took her days to wake up. She slept for days," he said.

"She didn't wake up at all?" Teari asked.

Jed's cheeks turned pink as he remembered slipping into her from behind, her soft hand edging him on. He controlled his mouth.

"You healed her just like we did the first time she broke her leg?" Teari asked.

"Yes."

"Something is off." Teari paced the room. "We need to open up the scar. The only problem is, she doesn't want us to."

"We must," Chel said. "We'll have to restrain her."

Jed was shaking his head. "She won't go for that."

"She must be healed," Chel argued.

"She will never forgive us for restraining her. It's not right." Jed was shaking his head. His relationship with Shay had been on shaky ground for a while. They'd both made promises to each other and broken them. He didn't want to lose her and he feared this would be the end of everything.

Jed rubbed his face. His stomach twisted. "I can erase her memory of it."

Chel frowned. "She explicitly told you to never do that."

"She'll leave if she remembers what we have

planned." Jed was shaking his head, feeling defeated. "I can't lose her."

The door slammed open and a giant Hellion entered the room. It was Skeele. He looked at Jed. "Do you know where your human is?"

"Sleeping," Jed said.

Skeele made a face. "Klaus just saw her scale the side of the castle and ride off into the forest on Nero's back." Skeele's brows rose. "What are you two going to do about that?"

Thirteen

Nero was running. He was faster than the wind. Faster than lighting. Faster than the speed of sound. His speed didn't scare Shay and Nero didn't worry about it frightening her like last time. He was definitely faster than when he'd rescued her at Clyburn's hovel. It felt like electricity was tingling under his skin as he galloped.

Shay's fingers twisted tight in Nero's mane as she held on. Fresh air brushed her face; it was still chilly, but it seemed winter was nearing an end. It smelled like springtime and burning embers. Shay felt alive for the first time in days. The anger and angst flowed off her back as Nero's hooves thudded on the ground. He galloped at a steady beat, a dark song, something archaic and intimidating like the sound of deep drums welcoming a sacrifice. His hoofbeats thrummed against dirt. The dead wandered nearby but never got close. Nothing came close to them.

Shay started telling Nero everything that had been going on. The broken leg, the fighting, Chel training her. She told her oldest friend everything and anything that came to mind.

Nero ran down broken streets. He ran between tall trees and down empty fields. He made a wide turn when Shay was done emptying her soul of all the chaotic thoughts that had been tormenting her. She felt lighter, freer, having all of that off her mind.

Nero slowed and paced in an empty grocery store parking lot.

Shay sat up straighter. "That felt good, boy." She rubbed Nero's neck.

Nero whinnied joyously. Nothing was better than having Shay back. Nothing. When he became the Crossroads Demon he feared he'd barely ever see her again. Fate had changed that. He was thankful to have her nearby every day.

"I don't know what to do," Shay said. "I'm not sure Jed really wants this. He's distant one minute, overprotective another." Shay shook her head and let her blue hair fly in the wind. "Maybe I should leave? Maybe we aren't meant to be together." Tears were welling behind Shay's eyes as she said it.

Nero weaved off the road and headed for the cemetery. He didn't have the words to help her, but he knew someone who might.

Shay recognized where they were. "It wasn't too long ago that I was here, playing house with Jed and Thrush." Shay took a deep breath and fought the pinching in her heart. It was the closest thing to normalcy they'd experienced. Jed let his guard down. He fell into bed with her every night and didn't hold back. It was just them. No one else. Until it wasn't. It seemed their relationship changed daily. Detours kept arising and driving a wedge between them. Just when Shay thought he was ready, something new caused him to second guess them.

"Hey, Shay." Noah waved from the other side of the fence. "What brings you out here?"

Shay jumped down from Nero's back and walked toward the gate. "I was just out getting some fresh air. I hope you don't mind that we stopped by."

"You're always welcome," a soft voice said.

Shay noticed Nightingale standing on the front stoop. "After everything you've done for our son, never worry about coming to visit."

Shay nodded, tears threatening to fall again. She didn't understand why she was so emotional.

"I know Thrush misses you," Nightingale said.

"Really?" Shay found that hard to believe since they'd only had a few weeks together.

Shay walked past the gate and Noah stayed, talking to Nero.

"Come on," Nightingale motioned for Shay to follow. "He's waking up from his nap."

Shay played on the floor with Thrush. She was sitting cross-legged with the little boy sitting on her lap. They played with wooden blocks. Shay whispered silly things to Thrush until he giggled and knocked the blocks over.

Nightingale was watching her. "Are you okay?" she asked.

Shay shrugged. "I'm not sure. Strange things have been happening and..."

"What kind of strange things?" Nightingale asked as she moved from the couch to the floor and scooted closer.

Shay told herself it wasn't because Nightingale could sense something off in Shay. Nightingale moved closer in a friendly way because she cared. That's what she repeated in her mind.

"I have a scar from my broken leg and Teari and Jed think there's some type of Demon poison stuck in it." Shay was rubbing her thigh.

"Noah told me a little bit about that."

Shay was looking down at the floor. "Last night at dinner... I ate nearly raw meat and liked it."

"That's not so concerning after being surrounded by Demons and half-breeds with blood bonds who drink each other's blood to stay alive. I'd say eating raw meat is the least of your concerns. Or at least it is in my opinion."

Shay laughed lightly. "Okay. My leg felt funny last night. Like it had changed shape."

"What kind of Demon poison is in your leg?" Nightingale asked.

"I don't know."

"Has a Demon injured you?"

"Nero kicked me and broke my leg. Twice. It was an accident."

Nightingale was nodding. "Have you been having nightmares?"

"Not that I can remember."

Nightingale pointed toward the door. "Your horse–"

"Nero. His name is Nero," Shay interrupted. "Sorry."

"He's a Demon. Never seen a horse Demon before. But you're both connected in some way."

Shay told Nightingale the story of how she'd found Nero in the field as a newborn foal covered in stings and barely alive. How she'd nursed him back to life and he had been her best friend ever since.

Nightingale was nodding in understanding as Shay spoke.

"You're both deeply connected. I know little about poisons and healing, but I could search your dreams and try to find some answers for you." Nightingale cleared her throat. "I try not to do it without permission these days. People get mad when I just show up."

Shay thought for a bit, staring out the window at Nero's black form pacing and eating grass. "Maybe that would give us some answers."

Fourteen

"DALK, you're assigned to dungeon duty tonight."

Alastor could barely believe his luck. He didn't even need to sneak into the castle, he was assigned to be there for the week.

Patience was a virtue he rarely possessed but the weeks of impersonating the Hellion recruit Dalk were paying off. All it took was one whisper to his commanding officer that he'd be grateful to be assigned guard duty. And bam, he was assigned. Alastor was floating on cloud nine as he ate dinner with the recruits then prepared to head to the castle. It was late in the evening as Alastor crossed the expanse of grass making his way to the dungeon entrance at the base of the mountain.

There was movement near the entrance. Alastor was

far enough away that he could watch it all unfold. Shay arrived on Nero. The horse trotted up to the door and Shay was throwing her leg over the side to get down when the Hellions blasted the door open. They grabbed Shay and dragged her off the horse. She fought as they carried her toward the entrance.

Don't damage my property, Alastor thought, wishing he could scold the Hellion who had his hands on her. He didn't want her bruised up and broken. Not unless it was by his hand.

He kept walking, reaching the lower entrance to the dungeon. He went inside.

Alastor felt cold prickle his skin. He turned to find a wisp of a woman watching him; black hair and ruby red lips. One moment she was there, the next she was gone. Alastor huffed. There was something familiar about her. He itched a scratch on his arm and kept walking.

Fifteen

"NO!" Shay was screaming at them. "Don't touch me!"

"This is to help you," Chel shouted back, baring sharp teeth to scare her into submission.

Shay kicked harder, panicked that they'd dragged her into the castle and down the hall to the infirmary without as much as a hello. It all felt very violating as they'd set her on an exam table and held her down. She'd done nothing wrong.

Jed was quiet as he held Shay's upper body.

"Make them stop, Jed!" Shay's eyes were wide with panic. "Make them stop!" Shay kicked until Chel grabbed her right leg and held it straight.

She swung her left foot around, kicked him in the side of the head and twisted her hips.

"Don't make me hurt you," Chel said.

"You are hurting me!" Shay yelled. "Let go!"

Chel grabbed her left ankle and held it down.

Teari walked closer with a pair of scissors. "I'm going to cut your jeans."

"No!" Shay was trying to twist her body, trying to get free, but Jed and Chel were stronger than her.

Tears streamed down Shay's face. She could feel her heart thrumming against her ribcage. She dragged air into her lungs. Warm breath puffed against her face. The room started spinning.

It sucked knowing that her relationship with Jed was over in this instant. He wasn't protecting her. He was in on their plan to cut her open against her will. Something broke in Shay. Something more than when her mother and father died at the ranch in Montana. It was broken and burning. It would never be the same. *They'd* never be the same.

The rough handling at the door pissed her off. This was worse. They didn't invite her to the infirmary once she'd returned. Chel and Klaus met her at the door and dragged her here. Jed showed up later, swapping places with Klaus. Shay hated that he was here. Hated that she was going to lose every ounce of trust she ever had for the man. She glanced at him while struggling. He was the most handsome man she'd ever met. She was sure his looks let him get away with plenty of shit. Not this time. She'd never trust a beautiful face again.

"This could all be for nothing," Teari warned. "The basilisk treatments have never worked on a human. I could find no record of it."

"We have to try," Jed pressed. "Whatever is stuck in her leg needs out."

"How could you?" Shay turned to Jed, loathing in her eyes. "How could you do this to me?"

Jed's mouth opened like he was going to say something.

Shay screamed as her jeans were cut and ripped.

"I'll make you forget," Jed promised. "You won't remember this." His features were like stone; uncaring.

"I hate you." Shay squeezed her eyes shut and tried to ignore the twisting sensation in her stomach. "Never touch me again."

"I'm sorry," Jed said. "It's for your own good."

Shay went still. Her head hurt but her stomach hurt more than ever. "You're lying to me again." She was looking at Jed. Crushed.

It felt like she was being stabbed through her heart and abdomen at the same time. Shay screamed as the pain in her stomach tightened and pulled. It yanked once, twice, three times and...

Shay disappeared.

Sixteen

Jed, Chel and Teari were staring at the empty cot in the infirmary.

"What just happened?" Chel asked. "Where did she go?" Chel started searching the room. "Shay!" He shoved cots and trays aside trying to find her. "She can't do that." Chel's eyes were like fire as he confronted Teari. "She's a human. She can't just disappear!"

"No. I suppose she can't." Teari set down the scissors she was using to cut Shay's jeans. She looked up at Jed.

"Did you do something to her?" Teari asked. "Did you change her?"

"Never," Jed promised. "I never changed her. I only promised to make her forget this." Both hands stretched through his hair and pulled at the ends as he paced away from the cot. "I only promised to make her forget me.

This. To forget any of this ever happened but she wouldn't let me. She forbade me from erasing her memories of me and sending her back to Montana."

Teari crossed her arms and stared at Jed. "You would make her forget? After all she's done? She helped save this realm by standing-in as Queen. She walked into a Safe House so Meg could get out. Shay saved you on the Earthen plane. She's quite possibly the strongest human I've ever met and yet you want to send her away. You want to make her forget? Is she deserving of this?"

"I must. To keep her safe. It's too dangerous here." Jed avoided Chel's gaze as the words came tumbling out of his mouth. The cement he'd used in his mind to keep his face straight while Shay had screamed at him was chipping and falling in chunks.

"I knew I could never trust you with her." Chel's voice was full of disgust.

The dam he'd put up was cracking and within seconds it all came tumbling down. Jed hated that he'd lied to her. Again. He betrayed her. Held her down in the infirmary and told her that he was going to wipe her memories. He wanted to puke. He pressed his hand to his stomach and tried to breathe but he couldn't. Something was blocking his throat. Something was squeezing him from the inside. He'd never felt so empty.

Suddenly heavy footsteps were coming at him. Jed

looked up to see Chel's rage filled expression. He leaned back on his knees accepting of his fate. Shay was gone. Jed had no reason to be here. He didn't know it before. He didn't realize how her lack of a presence would affect him. In this moment, he relished the blow that would send him elsewhere. He'd never accepted death so openly in his entire damned life.

Teari was fast when she leapt in Chel's path, humming blade of light drawn and ready.

"Don't," Teari warned Chel.

"We had one job and that was to protect her. Meg is gonna be pissed!" Chel was shouting, his deep voice echoing off the white walls of the infirmary.

"Leave me with him," Teari commanded.

Chel left, slamming the door so hard that wood shattered from the corners of the frame.

Teari turned on Jed. The flat of her foot struck him on the shoulder and he fell back onto the floor. Her mood shifted. Teari was a healer but she was also a warrior. The Archangel Gabriel would have no less as his personal healer.

"Is she dead?" Teari asked, blade ready.

Jed stared.

Teari took a deep breath. "I have had it up to here," she raised her hand above her head, "with you lovesick Angels."

"I'm not an Angel," Jed said.

"No shit. But it seems you've inherited the idiot half." Teari leaned closer to his face. "You have a bond with her. Search for her. Close your eyes and feel her just as closely as you feel her when you're taking her clothes off. Find that tether and follow it. Use a spell if you must."

Jed closed his eyes, his fingers tapped in spell casting. He whispered words that sounded like sunlight and rain and apology. *Her thread was there. Gold twisted with black.* Something wasn't right but she was there. He told Teari everything he saw.

"Is she dead?" Teari asked again.

"She's alive." Jed's eyes flashed open. "But she's not in Hell."

SEVENTEEN

AT THE CROSSROADS

IT WAS DARK. One minute Shay was screaming at Jed, the next she was gone, surrounded by night. Her head was spinning. She reached out to steady herself and felt something warm—soft hair. She blinked until her vision cleared and she heard the soft whinny of Nero footsteps on pea gravel. She no longer smelled woodsmoke or pine.

Nero was nudging her. She took the cue, climbed on his back, and tangled her fingers in Nero's mane.

"Where are we, boy?" she whispered.

Nero's teeth clicked. His only movement was a few steps forward then a few steps back.

Clouds cleared, and the moon illuminated their

surroundings. Shay noticed the ochre haze of Hell was gone. The air smelled fresh. The moonlight was milky.

"We're back on the Earthen plane. How did we get here?" she asked Nero.

"Thought you'd never get here," a deep voice said.

Nero turned.

Shay noticed markings on the road underneath them. Tension filled her body. She recognized the runes in a circular shape around them. They were trapped.

The man in front of them was dressed in a black suit. There was a black sports car parked on the side of the road. His shined shoes reflected moonlight.

Shay took in the four roads extending from the cross-roads she and Nero were trapped in.

"Never seen a Crossroads Demon as pretty as you," the man said, watching them warily. "Never seen a horse show up either."

Shay wasn't the Crossroads Demon. Nero couldn't talk, though. So Shay decided it was best for her to speak.

"What do you want?" Shay asked.

"A deal." The man rubbed his chin and watched her with dark eyes.

"What kind of deal?"

"Rebuilding after the war has become profitable for our company. I want you to kill my business partner."

"Why?"

"Money my dear."

"I'm not your dear." Shay narrowed her eyes.

"Will you make the deal or not?"

Shay nodded. "Your business partner."

"What do I give you in return?"

Shay's eyes flashed red. The tether that connected her to Nero went taut. The words that came out of her mouth were not of her own volition. They were compelled by the curse of the Crossroads Demon and Nero. "Out of the eater will come something to eat. And out of the strong will come something sweet."

Shay smiled and held out a dusky hand that was unfamiliar to her, one with long necrotic fingernails and a transparent golden ring on her middle finger.

"You want me to give you food?" the businessman asked.

"You said anything. Something sweet. Something to eat. Shake on it." Shay smiled wickedly. "Step into the circle," she taunted.

The businessman stepped forward, his back ramrod straight. He was trying to show calmness, but Shay could hear the rapid fluttering of his heart. Her mouth watered.

He held out a hand. Shay reached down from where she sat on Nero's back, her necrotic index finger scraped the soft inner skin of the businessman's wrist as they shook on it. Etched in darkness, the deal was done.

Nero reared up on his hind legs, hooves in the air. He whinnied, dark and ominous. A promise had been made and now the Crossroads Demon had to take care of business.

"Do you want his information?" the businessman stepped back, giving Nero more room.

"We know it all." Shay stared at the man. "Elias Corchran. Black hair. Fifty-two. Has a wife and three children, now teenagers. He'll be at a stoplight on Green Street in Marksville, Tennessee in eighty-four minutes. He will choke on his own blood after being ejected from the driver seat of his Dodge Ram pickup truck. He'll lay in the road for seven minutes as the EMTs fight traffic to get to him. After he dies you inherit a majority in the construction business you've been growing for ten years. Congratulations, Mr–"

Shay's head tipped as she realized he'd never introduced himself. She didn't need the information, she'd draw it from his soul. "Mr. Fremel. You're about to be a multi-millionaire."

The businessman took a few more steps back. "You know all that from our deal?"

"And more."

Now that the deal was done, Nero and Shay were released from the runes trapping them in the crossroads.

Nero shivered. His spine tingled as the transformation overtook him. He shivered, gnashed his teeth together, tensed his body, and changed. Nero was already huge but in that second he doubled in size, his long black tail and mane becoming stiff as needles and sharp as razorblades. His veins became giant ropes of obsidian, twining and swirling under his skin like protective armor.

"Holy shit," the business man muttered, backstepping as quickly as possible until he got to his car.

Shay changed. She didn't realize it. Her whole person had changed. Vision, form, morals. The poison in her scar allowed her to transform with Nero. They were a packaged deal now, their soul tether closer than ever. She was just as much of the Crossroads Demon as Nero was.

Shay clicked her tongue and Nero took off in the direction of Elias Corchran.

He galloped faster than the moonlight that was spilling over the Earthen plane. On his back, there was nothing but a shadow and a blue blur from Shay's hair.

Shay smiled wide as the crisp, cool air touched her skin and blew her hair behind her in a wave. There was nothing like a horse sprinting across an open plain. Shay remembered this feeling from life on the ranch. She leaned down and touched Nero's stiff mane. The sharp tines curled under her hands, providing grips. She held on tight as Nero ran. She wanted to laugh and shout and whoop into the night air. The thrall of running in the dark, free and unrestricted, filled her with dark energy.

Shay wasn't sure where they started their journey, she only knew the direction of Marksville, Tennessee.

Nero sprinted through forests, down empty roads, through towns and cities as nothing more than a shadow. Streetlights went black as he moved close but flickered back to life as he cleared them.

It felt like only minutes had passed when Nero slowed and Shay saw the sign for Marksville.

An engine revved as a dark blue truck sped down the road. A Dodge Ram. Elias slowed for the stoplight on Green Street. The light flicked to green. He sped up. Nero leapt into the intersection.

Elias saw the giant Demon horse but no one else did. They only saw the crash as he sideswiped the beast, veered to the side, and hit a pole. In a series of unfortunate events, his airbags failed–they had been filled with paper bags by the used car dealership he'd bought the truck from, and his seatbelt failed–the fabric and stitching tearing and releasing under the inertia of his body. Shay's head turned to watch Elias's body fly out the front window. He landed in the street with a sickening crack of bones and squelch of internal organs.

Nero wandered closer.

Blood spurted from Elias's mouth. He couldn't move with twenty-three broken bones including his cervical spine. Sirens blared in the distance. The ambulance company was having a rough night. This accident was one of ten in the past few hours. The crew was exhausted, the driver bleary-eyed as he took a wrong turn, delaying their response time by an extra four minutes. Those four minutes could have meant life. But for Elias, they simply helped sign his death certificate.

Nero backstepped into the shadows of an alley. Shay turned her head, listening to the *thump–thump–thump* as Elias's heartbeat slowed then finally stopped.

The golden rings on Shay and Nero's bodies glimmered with the transfer of power.

"Out of the eater will come something to eat. And out of the strong will come something sweet," Shay whispered the words.

She didn't know when they'd call upon Mr. Fremel to repay their deal. But they would call upon him eventually.

Nero and Shay's bodies shivered with anxious energy. "Let's do it again, boy." A dark smile quirked

Shay's lip. She clicked her tongue and kicked her heel against Nero's belly. "Hiya!"

Nero took off. He galloped through forests, across rivers and streams, up rocky hillsides and through mountain valleys. Shay thought the landscape resembled the southern Rockies with the snowcapped mountains.

Nero galloped into a valley clearing with a dark lake. The moon and stars were perfectly reflected, like a dark mirror. Nero bent to take a drink. A tingle ran down both their spines simultaneously and they transformed into their normal appearances.

There was a noise behind them. Shay reached for her weapon only to realize she didn't have one. She never had a chance to collect one before she was summoned out of Hell.

A large form walked toward them. Dark energy permeated from it, shadows curled around its legs and feet. Black feathers dragged against the grass in a continuous *shhhhh* sound. Shay recognized the wings. She recognized the feeling of him. This wasn't the first time they'd met. She knew him before he'd turned into this, helped him. She'd ridden in a car with him, guided him to safety.

It was Sparrow. The Raven King.

EIGHTEEN

Sparrow was staring, moonlight glittered in his eyes. A creature as alluring as Sparrow didn't belong in the valley between mountains. The beauty of nature was nothing compared to him. He was out of place. Or maybe, the scenic valley was out of place with Sparrow standing there.

"What are you doing here?" Shay asked.

"I could ask you the same thing." His head tipped to the side in a quirky movement. "Shay."

"Congratulations, you've remembered my name."

Silence passed.

"Does your Queen know that you're on the Earthen plane with your Demon hanging out? It's so... blasphemous." Sparrow was grinning.

"She's not my Queen." Shay held no alliances in the feud between Sparrow and Meg.

"Then why did you cover for her in that Safe House? The Deacons told me what you did. Impersonated the Queen of Hell. Why would a little human girl do that?" He took one step forward, hands hung unsuspecting at his sides.

Shay stood her ground. "It was the right thing to do."

Sparrow smiled charmingly, showing teeth. He glanced away from her, his focus on Nero. "Never seen a Demon horse before." He looked at her again, taking her in. "Never seen a Demon *human* before. Only recognized the blowtorch blue hair when I saw the blur running across the Earthen plane. Could never forget a human like you."

"We were summoned." Shay crossed her arms and lifted her chin. Sparrow's form was imposing but she was sure he would not hurt her. And Shay sure as shit would not take threats from a man who was quite fucked in the head since the first time she'd met him. Sure he was a King from the Seven Kingdoms of Heaven, that didn't mean his brain was right. Something was twisted in him. Twisted and broken.

"I heard a rumor that a human girl killed an Angel mid-air, which is impressive." Sparrow's wings relaxed.

Shay shrugged.

"And then the bell tolled for the Crossroads Demon pact." Sparrow's chin dipped. "You have blood on your hands now."

"I'm not the only one."

"How did you get in this situation?"

Shay shook her head, blue hair flying. "I don't know."

But she did know, she knew that she had Demon poison in her scar. She would not tell Sparrow that.

"There are rules. Didn't the Deacons tell you?"

"I haven't spoken with any Deacons," Shay said.

"That's probably a good thing given Meg's *situation*. I'm sure if another showed up at her door she'd slaughter them like she did that poor Hellion recruit."

"How do you know about that?" Shay asked. Narrowing her eyes, she noted every tick in his face, every quirk, every flash of teeth.

"Word gets around." Sparrow's hand went to his pocket. He sighed. "So, whose side are you going to choose?"

"That's none of my business," Shay said. The only side she'd chosen was Jed's. Now she wasn't so sure about all that.

"Oh you're too naïve. You must choose a side in a war like this."

"You told the Deacons you'd truced. The war is over."

"The war never ends. And what I said doesn't make a difference to the side you've chosen."

"I didn't choose a side."

"But you're doing Demon work now." Sparrow wagged his finger. "That has to be breaking a rule of some kind. There's never been a human doing the things you've just done."

Shay chuckled. "Have you spent any time on the Earthen plane? Humans can be pretty despicable. The things they can do to each other..." Shay threw her hands in defeat. "It's not by my choice. I didn't make a choice to do this."

"But you refused the choice to fix it."

Shay blinked and closed her mouth. Sparrow knew too much. He shouldn't know what goes on behind closed doors in Hell.

"Who told you that?"

Sparrow motioned to her. "You're clearly here. Your Queen would not have allowed this to continue. We all know Teari has been visiting Meg's realm. It's easy putting the puzzle together. And your reaction solidifies my speculations."

"She's not my Queen. How many times do I need to tell you?"

"Everyone chooses." His head tipped to the side and he blinks. "How's that half-Angel you were tagging around with?" Sparrow held his arms out showing the black, twisting runes. "I might need him to refresh my ink."

"I'm not sure he'll take kindly to you threatening me."

Sparrow laughed, his face turned to the starry night sky until he'd finished, then finally he looked at her again. "I didn't come here to threaten you, Shay. I'm just catching up with an old friend. I'll never forget you and Jed guiding me to safety. You guided me straight to Meg and changed *everything*."

He was suddenly too close to her. In an instant he'd moved and she'd barely seen it. His shadows curled around her feet. Two feathers broke loose of his wings and floated through the air. One landed on her shirt.

Nero made a noise that sounded like a growl, his snout pushing over her shoulder. He was ready to call upon the change if need be.

Sparrow glanced up at Nero. His smile dropped. "You have a leash for that thing?"

"He's a free horse." Shay looped her arm around Nero's head and pet him. "He does what he wants."

Sparrow reached out and grabbed the black feather off Shay's shirt. He twirled it between his fingertips, then slid the soft edge of it against her cheek. "Hold onto this, Shay-baby. It might come in handy one day."

He was standing in her space, his green eyes boring into hers. He smelled good and she could feel the heat from his body. Jed had warned her about Sparrow. Warned her to stay away from him and she was realizing why. The Raven King was a spectacle. He was a black hole that drew you in. Mesmerizing. His voice was like warm whiskey. Shay wanted to touch him. It was hard being this close, hard to look away. He was too hand-some. Moreso than that Angel she killed. Moreso than Jed, and she hated to admit that.

Shay wanted to bare her neck in offering. She couldn't control the urge. She closed her eyes and felt Sparrow tuck the feather into the pocket of her jeans. His fingers pressed against her hip.

"Stop what you're doing," Shay warned.

"Be careful, Shay-baby," Sparrow was whispering in her hear. "I'd hate to see Meg pay for what's happening to you."

"My choice," Shay said. "Stop calling me Shay-baby."

When her eyes flashed open, Sparrow was gone and only wisps of black shadows remained. Shay shivered, feeling cold without his warm body next to her.

"Fuck," she shouted to the night.

Nero whinnied in agreement.

Nineteen

Shay woke up in the suite, alone, her body aching. She was exhausted. She felt like she'd been hit by a truck.

Somehow she'd returned to Hell. She didn't remember crossing the Veil or a portal. She rubbed her face and rolled out of bed. Her neck was sore–Sparrow. Shay ran to the bathroom, her hand against the soft skin of her neck. She couldn't feel any scars marking her skin. Shay flicked on the light and leaned toward the mirror, checking her skin. She released a breath when she didn't see any bite marks.

Shay had never known Sparrow like that. The dude was a nutcase last time she was in his presence. But that Sparrow... it was no surprise Meg had fallen so hard for him. Shay thought about the scars on Jed's neck from Meg and his reaction to her having bitten him. Shay wondered if she'd feel the same about Sparrow's bite, pissed off but enchanted.

She wandered the suite. Jed wasn't there. Her skin ached and prickled. Shay rubbed her arms trying to quell the sensation. Her shoulder brushed against the doorway and it worsened. Shay paused and touched the doorway again. Her skin prickled like a thousand ants were crawling on her.

The runes.

Shay found a sponge in the kitchenette, wet it, and began scrubbing the suite. She started with the largest rune on the floor by the door. With every one that she erased, the prickling of her skin eased. She scooped up the lines of salt and threw them down the sink. Shay scrubbed the walls. She took a knife, then a marker to the doorways and damaged Jed's intricately drawn and carved markings.

When she was done, the room looked less chaotic and Shay felt like she could finally breathe. Her skin calmed and felt warm. She turned when the door opened.

Shay wasn't sure how she was going to react to seeing Jed again after he'd held her down in the infirmary. She wanted to slap him for promising to erase her memories. She wanted to kiss him because she'd missed him. Something melted in her when she saw him. It always did. She was drawn to him just as badly as he was drawn to her.

He looked tired, his hair falling loose from where it was tied behind his neck.

"You're back." Jed closed the door and stood unmoving. "Where did you go?"

Shay shook her head. "I... I don't know."

"What happened?"

She brushed salt off her arm before walking to the sink and washing her arms under the tap.

"Where have you been, Shay?" Jed asked again.

"I said, I don't know." Her back was to him. She turned.

"Were you in Hell? A different plane? How did you disappear like that?" His eyes were searching her face for truth, for something to hold on to. Nothing was right between them anymore. "Tell me, Shay." He rubbed his face, startled when he noticed the changes to the suite.

"No. No, no, no." Jed turned, taking in the bare walls and scratched door frames. "What did you do?" he shouted.

"They were making me sick." Shay crossed her arms.

"How? You're human. There's nothing supernatural about you. You're not an Angel or a Demon. How could they make you sick?"

Shay scratched her thigh absently. It hurt. His true

thoughts were coming out. She was nothing special. Just a human. She'd saved his life battling an Angel on the Earthen plane but that wasn't enough for him. She was nothing special in his eyes.

"Where's my marker?" Jed started searching the kitchen drawers.

"Gone." Shay felt no remorse over what she'd done.

"Where are they?" Jed was rifling through drawers, panicked. "I had a whole bunch."

"I threw them out the window."

Jed stilled. "Why would you do that?"

"Hurts like a bitch, doesn't it?" Shay's face twisted, her chin trembled. "Losing all your trust in someone you thought you loved." She felt tears burning her eyes.

"You never said you loved me."

"Would that even make a difference?" Shay asked. "Would *love* have stopped you from lying to me? From holding me down so they could cut me open?"

Jed was staring, his eyes bleary. He already hated himself. Hearing the accusation from her lips made it worse; made it real. All he'd ever wanted was some normalcy.

"Shay," Jed said. "You are not yourself."

"Maybe I *like* it," she bit back through clenched teeth. "Maybe I enjoy not being weaker than everyone around me."

Tension filled the room. The energy was vibrating. Shay's heart beat against her ribs. She wanted to touch him. She moved closer. Her hands slid up his chest and around his neck, her fingers twisting in his hair. She kissed him, gently at first, exploring his body while they were both angry and on edge.

He pulled back. "You said you hated me."

Shay kissed him again, harder this time; punishing.

Jed matched her. His tongue entered her mouth and twined with hers.

She pulled away, out of breath, lips swollen and aching. "You lied to me."

"You told me to never touch you again," Jed reminded her.

"Well... now that you're standing in front of me looking like you do..." Her eyes wandered up and down, taking him all in. "Clearly you're feeling miserable about what you did to me." His hair was tousled, his shirt torn. He obviously hadn't slept since she disappeared. If anything he'd been razing Hell trying to find her.

That's what she told herself. He'd searched everywhere for her. She searched his eyes and found torment staring back at her.

Shay's hands moved over his shirt and tore it down the center. Her lips never left his. Her palms pressed against his hot skin, feeling the ridges and planes of his body.

Jed's hands were in her hair, holding her as he kissed her deeply, his tongue working against hers, his teeth nipping at her lips.

Shay's hands went to the waist of his pants and tugged, knuckles brushing against hot skin. She felt him tense.

Jed moaned into her mouth. His fingers pressed against her skull in silent plea.

She unbuttoned. Unzipped.

"Fuck," Jed murmured as he kicked his pants off. He stiffened.

"Don't," Shay begged. "Don't freeze up on me. I can't stand it." She reached down and took him in her hand, stroking, squeezing lightly.

Jed shuddered and closed his eyes as his hands trailed down her neck, down her chest to press against her breasts. He gripped her waist and lifted her.

Shay's legs wrapped around his waist and she held onto his shoulders as he moved to the couch. He lowered her feet to the ground, tearing her shirt like she'd done to him, but faster, harder, jerking her body. The thrill was electric, the heat burning.

"Christ." Shay was kicking off her boots and pulling

her pants down. She shoved Jed until he fell back on the couch, looking up at her.

Shay blinked, wanting to remember this moment with him, looking up at her like she was an Angel, like she was something more than human. A shiver ran up her spine as she gazed at his body, hard and waiting for her.

"From this moment on," Shay said as she straddled him, "you promise me. Never hold me down against my will again." She licked his mouth and lifted her hips, her hand between them, touching his hardness; moving up and down, painfully slow.

Jed hissed, sucking in a breath. "You're going to kill me."

"I might." Shay smirked. "Promise."

"Never again." His gaze was dark, true.

Jed whispered something that sounded like ice clinking in a whiskey glass. Her underwear fell away. His fingers brushed down her body, taking in every curve before dipping between her legs and stroking her.

Shay let out a shaky breath, her hands moving to his shoulders to steady herself. "Oh, God..." Shay moaned as he pressed his finger between her folds. She shuddered as he circled.

Shay kissed his neck, his collarbone, the soft skin below his ear. She was so close. His fingers moved away and Jed gripped her hips and lowered her body against his. In a slick movement, he pressed inside her. Her body stilled at the ache.

"You always wait too long." Shay leaned back as she adjusted, slowly taking his length and thickness into her body. "We should do this twice a day, every day."

Jed smirked, palms rubbing over her nipples, his hips pressed up. "I'm trying to be better than the Hellions."

"I'm not asking for blood." Shay bit her lip as he rubbed against her inner walls.

"You just want my body?" His hands moved to her hips again and squeezed. He held her still against him and sat up straight, focusing on the door behind Shay's shoulder.

The movement was right. Shay moaned, her mouth went to his collarbone. She licked and kissed and sucked as he dragged against her. She wanted to answer him but she couldn't think straight.

"Someone is here."

"Let them wait." Shay shifted her hips, forcing him deeper and moaning with pleasure.

There was a loud thud as the door to the suite blasted open.

Twenty

Alastor entered Shay's suite easily with one solid kick to the door, surprised that there were no protection spells or fancy locks. He chuckled to himself with how easy it was and laughed louder when he saw Shay and that half-breed fucking on the couch.

He'd never seen her naked when they were at the camp. For the one moment in his life he'd given her privacy in the cabin shower. He shouldn't have.

Shay was a prize to look at; all smooth skin, curves, and muscle. The long, blue hair did it though. She was small compared to Demon females, this would be easy.

Jed chanted a spell and they were clothed again. He scrambled forward and shoved Shay behind him.

"Exactly who I was looking for," Alastor said. "We meet again." He showed sharp teeth and glared.

"You're dead," Jed said, his fingertips sparking as he drew energy.

"Wrong." Alastor looked to Shay and smiled. "You both have a debt to pay."

Alastor went after Jed, blade drawn and malice on his face.

The men fought, but the space was too small. Fists flew. Walls cracked. Furniture was turned to toothpicks as Jed blasted Alastor with battle magic. Nothing stopped the Demon. His Hellion uniform was ripped. His arm was bleeding.

The air crackled with tension as Jed and Alastor locked eyes, each prepared to do whatever it took to emerge victorious in this deadly game.

Shay stood between them, her presence a tantalizing prize coveted by Alastor, her eyes reflecting a mixture of fear and determination as she braced herself.

With a flick of his wrist, Jed summoned tendrils of arcane energy, crackling with raw power, to encircle Shay protectively. His eyes blazed with determination as he prepared to defend her against the malevolent force that threatened to tear her from his grasp. She'd only just returned, he needed more time to make it right between them, to show her that he'd do better.

Alastor was a creature of darkness and deceit; he grinned wickedly as he brandished a basilisk tooth knife, its jagged edges glinting ominously in the subdued light of the suite. With a predatory gleam in his eyes, he advanced toward Shay, his intentions clear as he sought to claim her for his own dark purposes.

The air filled with the clash of magic and malice as Jed and Alastor engaged in a deadly dance of power and peril. Spells crackled through the air, weaving intricate patterns of light and shadow as they clashed with thunderous force. The tendrils slammed into Alastor's chest, throwing him back and cracking a wall. As plaster showered the room, Alastor sprang to his feet and launched himself at Jed, knife ready.

Alastor's movements were swift and unpredictable as he dodged Jed's attacks with uncanny agility. With each strike of the basilisk tooth knife, he carved through the protective barriers that Jed summoned, inching closer to his prize.

Shay was caught in the crossfire. She was trying to get to the bedroom to get her pistol or hunting knife but every time she made a move, the fighting men blocked her. She picked up a broken chair leg and held it like a batter at the box, ready for action. She watched as the two men collided with terrifying ferocity. Her heart ached with fear for Jed's safety.

The room smelled of dust and sweat and blood as the chaos continued. Energy flew from Jed's hands, hit the window, and broke it. Shay ducked to avoid the spray of glass.

Jed tripped on a piece of broken table.

Alastor seized his opportunity, took the moment to leap forward, arm raised, Basilisk tooth blade ready. With swift and decisive blow, the knife found its mark with deadly precision. The blade sunk in Jed's chest, the tip landing directly into his heart.

"No!" Shay screamed as she ran toward Jed. "No, no, no!" He didn't move. Never took a final breath. He wasn't struggling. Something wasn't right.

Alastor seized his opportunity, picking up the chair leg and advancing on Shay.

Something hit Shay in the back of the head. All she saw was a bright light then darkness. She didn't even feel Alastor dragging her across the floor then throwing her over his shoulder.

The room fell silent as Jed finally took his last breath and it echoed amongst the debris.

TWENTY-ONE

SHAY COULDN'T MOVE. She was strapped to a table, thick leather wrapped around her wrists and ankles. Coarse wood scraped her back as she struggled to get free. Shay dragged air into her lungs, did her best to ignore the sharp pull of pain in her ribs.

Footsteps came closer; hollow sounding. Heavy. She recognized the large man, the scruffy beard, the shadows that seemed to shift on his face.

Alastor.

"You're dead." Shay's eyes went wide, terrified. "I watched you die."

Alastor laughed, deep and booming from down in his chest. "I am very hard to kill, Shay."

He was touching her bare ankle. Shay's heart was

thrumming in her chest. She was wearing nothing. "Stop," she said.

Alastor's hand stopped mid-calf and he twisted her leg so he could see all of the scar along her thigh. His eyes traced the ragged red edge of it.

"Oh, dear, little human." He sniffed her leg. "This is something different." His large hand circled just above her knee, holding her leg still as he touched the raised scar with his free hand. Nails drifted over her skin drawing goose bumps. Dark eyes met hers.

"Let me go," Shay said, tugging at the leather binding her wrists. "You killed him!" Shay could barely process everything that was happening. The last thing she saw was Alastor stabbing Jed and a pool of blood.

Alastor chuckled. "Doubt he's dead. That knife can't kill a half-breed like him," he shook his head and clicked his tongue. "It only incapacitated him long enough for me to get away with my prize."

Alastor's fingers rubbed soft skin. "No. No, I don't think I will let you go. You and that half-breed Angel cost me everything. And now you're going to pay me back for eons worth of work." He exhaled loudly. "So much was lost when you all got in the mix. You cannot imagine what you disrupted."

"I don't have any money." Shay struggled, this time shifting her feet against the straps holding her ankles.

Alastor laughed, his deep voice echoing throughout the walls of the hovel. "You won't be paying me back in money." He squeezed her scarred thigh.

"I have nothing," Shay said, watching him warily.

He smiled and it was devious.

Alastor reached for the metal handle of a fire poker. The end was red-hot. It wasn't a poker, Shay realized. It was a brand like the one her daddy used to mark the cows that belonged to the ranch. Shay knew exactly what that was. Alastor was going to mark her as his and judging from the shape of the rune, she would have a very hard time escaping him.

"This way, you'll always come back to me." Alastor's eyes reflected the flame in the fireplace as he searched her bare body for the right place to burn her.

TWENTY-TWO

Nero felt a tug along the thread that connected to Shay. Something was wrong. She was frightened and hurt. Nero moved to his feet and paced under her window.

He whinnied, loud. Then again louder. She didn't come to the window.

He stomped his hooves and snorted.

More fear tore down the thread. She was terrified. He rose on his hind legs and slammed his front hooves down on the outer wall of the castle. Shards of stone flew into the air, rocks fell around him.

It was moments like this that he wished he could speak. He whinnied louder, his eyes wide.

Shay never came.

Nero had been on the royal grounds long enough to

know where certain people were during the day. He ran to the Hellion training grounds to find Skeele and Chel. Those two were the most protective of Shay.

Nero galloped, his heavy body leaving deep hoof-prints in the field and kicking up clumps of grass.

Nero interrupted Skeele as he spoke to three rows of Hellions. He ran right between them, blocking Skeele with his gigantic body.

"Get out of here." Skeele shoved at Nero.

Nero nickered and huffed.

The Hellion Commander was becoming more annoyed as Nero tried to get his attention and communicate that something was wrong. Skeele kept pushing the horse away and baring sharp teeth. Skeele was reaching for his blade.

"Come here, Nero," Chel interrupted.

"Get that damned creature off the training grounds. I'll cast him off this land if he can't control himself," Skeele threatened.

Chel made a clucking sound and motioned for Nero to follow.

"You're going to get your ass tossed out of here, beast." Chel crossed his arms and stared.

Nero's eyes were wide as he dragged his head toward the castle over and over again.

"Is it Shay?" Chel asked.

Nero whinnied loudly.

"Show me."

Nero ran toward the castle in the burning caves. Chel ran, keeping a steady pace behind him.

Nero motioned toward Shay's window with his muzzle. He snowed his teeth and widened his eyes.

Chel rubbed his chin. "I'm going inside."

Chel made his way to the door of the castle. He ran down the hall that led to the winding stairway. Then up he went, taking three steps at a time. Something wasn't right. He sniffed the air. Someone who didn't belong had been here.

Heavy footsteps echoed behind him.

Chel turned to see Skeele running up the stairs.

"What happened?" Skeele asked.

"Something is not right," Chel gripped his blade.

"Meg!" Skeele ran for Meg's room.

Chel followed. He was sure the problem wasn't Meg, but he had a duty to protect her first. Meg's wing was undamaged.

Skeele shoved Meg's bedroom door open.

Chel saw her sitting on the balcony, whistling to a yellow songbird. He left Skeele and ran down the opposite end of the hall.

He was right. The door to Shay and Jed's suite was broken to pieces and strewn across the floor.

"Shay?" Chel called. Unease filled his gut. This was very bad. He'd been in this suite enough to know that runes were missing. Jed was so neurotic he'd marked every wall, every door and window. There was less magic here than before.

"Shay? Are you here?" Chel asked. He could hear Nero making noise below the window.

Furniture was broken. There were holes in the walls. Chel followed the worst of the damage. There was blood everywhere. Chel held a hand to his face, fought the desire to lick it off the floorboards. He found the cause of all the gore.

Jed was lying in a pool of blood, a Basilisk tooth blade jabbed through his chest.

"Fuck." Chel ran to Jed and pulled out the blade of Basilisk tooth. He hadn't seen one of those since he was a child.

Once the bone was out, Jed's eyes flickered open. The milky dullness cleared. The wound in his chest began healing from a quickly whispered charm.

"What the fuck was that?" Jed's voice croaked.

Chel inspected the weapon in his hand. "Something old." He tucked the blade in his pocket for later inspection. "Something I've only heard about in fairytales."

"Hell has fairytales?" Jed quipped.

Chel shrugged. "Where's Shay?" He snapped as he

began searching the bedroom. He tore the sheets off the bed, flipped the mattress, pulled down the curtains. He slammed open the door to the closet then the bathroom.

"She's not here," Jed confessed. "Someone took her."

"Are you sure it was someone? Or was it the poison?" Chel asked.

"No. No." Jed held up a hand as he moved slowly to stand. "It was Demon dressed as a Hellion. We've come across him before on the Earthen plane. I killed him months ago." Jed shook his head. "How is he still alive? How was he a Hellion recruit?"

"How did you kill him?" Chel asked.

Energy crackled from Jed's fingertips. "Archaic light."

Chel released a cold snicker. "If that Demon did not die by light, he must die by fire." Chel headed for the doorway. "You didn't kill him the first time and now he has found his way back to you and taken Shay. Is that what you're telling me?"

Jed was collecting weapons, changing his torn shirt, and slinging his bag of supplies over his shoulder as he replied, "It appears so."

"Perfect." Chel led Jed down the hall. "It's been a while since I killed something." He cracked his knuckles. "We will hunt it."

———

Chel was conversing with Skeele and the other Hellions as Jed selected another blade from the wall of weapons in the Hellion lounge.

There was a loud knock on the door and Teari let herself in.

The warriors and Jed turned to face her.

"She has Crossroads Demon poison in her." Teari's face was perfectly still as she tried to explain the seriousness of the situation. "Nero has it on his hoofs just like any other Crossroads Demon would have on their claws. It's just like the injury he had on his flank that we had to heal with the basilisk."

"So heal her," Chel said.

Teari shook her head. "It's not that easy. The basilisk doesn't take to humans, we saw that. And her wound is closed. There is poison trapped in the scar tissue."

"Cut it out. That's what you wanted to do before," Skeele said, glaring like he had no time for this side-quest.

Teari was shaking her head. "That was before I knew what it was. It could spread if we cut wrong. Then it would go throughout her body. If it's in the scar tissue, then it's contained for the most part. If it gets into her blood, we have a bigger problem."

"But she is not the same. She's not right," Jed said.

"You could have her like this, with a little darkness she can control most of the time. Or she could turn into something completely different," Teari explained. "Right now, she's still Shay. She might get called off to do some Crossroads Demon work with Nero, but it's still Shay deep down. If that poison gets released into her whole body, we have no idea what she'll turn into or if she'll survive. You could lose her. Forever."

The realization hit Jed like a freight train. His breath hitched. He'd imagined freeing Shay from this nightmare. It seemed slightly innocent if by his hands, on his terms. Jed would have control over saying goodbye. That false dream would come to a quick end. Jed didn't like the feeling of having no control. He'd spent too much of his life without control.

Jed flexed his fists.

Teari's gaze fell to the motion.

"Where is she?" Teari asked. "I have to speak with her."

"That's going to be kinda hard," Jed said. "She's been kidnapped."

"By whom?" Teari walked closer to the men, searching their faces, unafraid to challenge them. "Who took her?"

"A Demon named Alastor," Chel said.

Teari paled as she glanced to Jed and he didn't like what he saw in the depths of her irises. "You're going to get her?"

"Yes," Jed tucked the knife in his belt. "We're leaving now."

Nero was waiting at the door as Jed and Chel exited. Skeele wouldn't risk sending any more Hellions. Meg was with child and that put her at risk. He didn't want to let Chel go, but the Hellion argued until Skeele gave in.

"Of course you're here," Chel said to Nero. "Let's go."

Jed reached out as Nero nuzzled his shoulder, urging him on. "Thanks, boy."

The trio left the royal grounds, headed to find Shay and kill the Demon who took her.

TWENTY-THREE

Teari stood before King Gabriel. She had returned to the Seven Kingdoms of Heaven. Something wasn't sitting right in her gut. She'd worked hard to figure out what was afflicting Shay and combined with Meg's pregnancy, the demands from both realms were draining her. She needed guidance.

Gabriel was one of the original Archangels, one of the few surviving that Meg hadn't killed. He was also Meg's father.

Gabriel raised overgrown brows as Teari approached him, smelling like brimstone. Gabriel recognized it.

"What?" he asked.

"Something strange is happening in Hell." Teari sat with Gabriel and poured herself a glass of water from the tray in front of her.

"Something strange is always happening there since Meg took over." Gabriel scratched his beard absently.

Teari took a long drink and collected her thoughts. "Have you heard of a Demon called Alastor?"

Gabriel's enormous form stilled for the slightest instant. "Perhaps."

"I'm trying to decide if I should involve the Deacons."

"That's not your call," Gabriel reminded her. "Meg hates when they meddle."

Teari tapped long fingers against the glass. "A human is involved."

Gabriel looked bored. "They better get it to a Safe House."

"This human is not dead. It's the one from Meg's trial."

Gabriel had been there for Meg's tribunal with the Deacons. "They didn't seem to care about her months ago. She's harmless."

Blue eyes searched her face. Gabriel was the most neutral of all the Archangels but he knew if the others got wind of a human still traipsing around Hell, that would give the Deacons and the Seven Kingdoms of Heaven another reason to meddle with Meg.

Gabriel sighed. "We've only had a few blissful months of silence on all realms."

"It was wonderful." Teari pushed the glass away, her stomach feeling queasy. "So you know Alastor?"

Gabriel nodded, solemnly.

"Who is he?"

"Clea's brother."

Dread filled Teari. If Alastor was Clea's brother, that meant Alastor was Meg's uncle. She probably didn't even know. He could challenge her for the throne.

Clea couldn't take the throne because she was a ghost but she could forewarn her daughter.

"I must inform her," Teari said as she stood.

Gabriel grabbed her wrist. "Leave it alone."

"But she's your daughter."

Gabriel shook his head. "I know."

A million terrible scenarios were running through Teari's mind. Meg had killed Lucifer in a moment of rage and unexpectedly took the throne of Hell. No one had challenged Meg, yet. None of the Archangels were happy with Meg taking the throne. The Deacons seemed impassive, as usual. The inhabitants of Hell were under control, as much as wild Demons and the dead could be controlled. But now Alastor was close enough to kidnap someone from inside the castle. This was a change that Teari never saw coming.

"I need air," Teari said as she launched from her chair and ran out of Gabriel's house. She ran past freshly painted walls, workers cleaning windows, art that had been on display for eons. She shoved open the newly constructed door that had been replaced after the Fast-Zombie War. Fresh air hit her face as she ran down the steps of the porch. White wings burst from her back and Teari took to the air like an uncaged lion. She flew straight up, until the sun burned her face. She turned, gazing down. From this distance she could see the Raven King's lands and the glittering of Babylon. She didn't know where to go or who could help.

Teari held up her hands, remembering a time when she didn't have any, when she'd been bitten by the dead and nearly died, and Meg *saved* her. She owed a debt to Meg. A life debt. She wasn't sure what Alastor had planned but Teari knew that the balance between realms was fickle and delicate and this was the first time in ages that they'd found peace.

Teari tilted her body, positioning herself to dive-bomb to the nearby forest. She dropped from the sky like an eagle and landed near Sparrow's old cabin on Gabriel's land.

The door was unlocked. Teari let herself in and the memories flooded her, memories of the time when Sparrow was Gabriel's Legion Commander. A time before he'd gone to Hell to do his time as a Hellion to clear his family's curse before he'd been let loose upon the Earthen plane as a shadow to cause unbalance and chaos. It had all changed so much. Teari paced the cabin. She couldn't do much. Yes, she was an Archangel's daughter, but she'd joined Gabriel's kingdom. Her father was no ally. She rubbed her face. She and the Raven King had been friends long ago. They'd been on the same team. Teari needed a friend like Sparrow again. She gazed at the long forgotten bookshelf lined with books about birds. The only problem was, Sparrow was not the man he used to be and Teari doubted he'd help his archenemy. But maybe... maybe if there was something in it for him.

TWENTY-FOUR

CHEL WAS POINTING to a drop of blood on the road. "She's bleeding." He sniffed. "This way."

Jed didn't need to track her the way Chel was. He'd whispered a spell that showed him the direction Alastor was travelling.

Chel watched the wisps of Alastor moving through time. The Demon was carrying Shay over his shoulder and running. Shay looked like a child in comparison. The Demon was fast and strong but Chel wasn't scared. He'd kill the Demon in a heartbeat. He swore he wouldn't let the male darkness that ended his sister's life reach Shay. At least this time there was no surprise, they had a trail to follow.

"Showoff," Chel grumbled as the wisps of magic disappeared.

"Where is he going?" Jed asked.

"Probably the mountains." Chel waved ahead of them. "It's far." Chel glanced at Jed, judgingly. "Would be easier if you could move faster." He held out his arms. "I could carry you."

"Not on your life, buddy."

Jed pulled his spell book from a pocket and flipped through the pages, looking for something that might help them. He'd become better with his magic these past few months. There was a time when he'd have to pull out the spell book daily. Now it was rare, but he kept it on him.

Nero kept nudging Jed's shoulder. Every so often the horse would gallop ahead of the men and look back expectantly, like they were going far too slow for Nero's liking. Nero would huff and paw at the road, urging them to move faster. Finally, Nero stopped in front of Jed and when Jed tried to sidestep, Nero nudged him with his flank.

"What's gotten into you, boy?" Jed reached out and raked his hand over Nero's shoulder.

"Not one for signals are ya, man?" Chel asked. "Not surprised."

Jed threw him a confused look.

"Nero wants you on his back. We'll move a lot faster if you ride him."

"It's been a while." Jed jumped, threw a leg over Nero's back, and gripped his mane.

Nero shook his head and whinnied what sounded like an exasperated "*finally*."

"I think he wants you to hold on," Chel chuckled as he took two steps then launched himself into the air.

Nero neighed wildly before tipping his head down and taking off.

Jed startled, nearly fell, before he leaned forward and held on for dear life. Wind whipped his face. Jed had never ridden a horse or any beast that moved as fast as Nero. The rescue crew of three moved much faster this way. Chel flew overhead, his strong bat-like wings propelling him through the air. Nero held back with how fast he wanted to run. He knew Jed wasn't used to his speed and didn't want to lose the man. But he was fast, so fast Chel laughed from the sky as he beat his wings. It was a race like never before. Wings beating, hooves clomping. The pair of Demons beat the air and the road like it was their playground. The sound of it sent creatures of Hell scattering to avoid them.

Chel's face split into a childlike grin. Nero showed his teeth and flared his nostrils with the reminiscent memory of freedom running through the mountains on the Earthen plane. It was electric. The feeling of being a savior was like nothing else.

TWENTY-FIVE

ALASTOR PRESSED the red-hot branding poker to Shay's hip. Her skin sizzled and smoked.

Shay screamed at the top of her lungs. Skin along her wrists and ankles tore as she surged against the leather bindings. Tears fell from her cheeks. She wanted nothing more than to escape but she was trapped, tied to this shitty table like a hog for butchering.

"That's lovely. Scream for me." Alastor was enjoying this too much. "You'll scream later too." He was staring at the vee of her thighs. "You'll scream every day for me."

"You're a fucking pig." Shay spit on him and tried to wiggle away from the scorching pain of the branding tool.

Alastor slapped one massive hand down on her pelvis to hold her in place. He was a giant to her. His hand spanned her from hipbone to hipbone as he braced her. "We're almost finished." He licked his lips. "Want this to burn you good and deep so you never forget what you cost me."

The branding hurt worse than anything, worse than breaking her leg. There was something about the smell of singed skin and the bone deep pain that sent Shay over the edge. She knocked her head against the table, trying to focus elsewhere but it just hurt so damn bad. Her hands curled into fists, still pulling against the restraints.

When it finally stopped, Shay's body ached. Tears soaked her hair. Metal clanged as Alastor tossed the branding tool aside and scrutinized his work.

The mark on Shay's hip was bright red. Blood dripped down her hip. Alastor swiped a finger across her skin, collecting the blood, and brought it to his lips.

"Mmmmm." Alastor closed his eyes as he tasted her blood. "Wow." His eyes flashed open and Shay could see the red return. Shadows danced across his cheekbones. He shook a finger at her. "Never thought you'd taste like that. Familiar. Human... but there's something else there."

Something flashed across his face; control.

Shay was looking at the brand on her hip wishing it would heal. She wasn't sure she'd be able to walk if she ever got free. She was sure he'd branded her bone.

Shay turned, feeling something sharp against her thigh. She tried to move her leg but Alastor gripped it, twisting, the tip of his knife circling her scar.

"What is this?" Alastor tapped on the disfigured skin. He seemed genuinely curious.

"I broke my leg. The bone was sticking through." Shay's words came out staccato and breathy as she fought the pain from her deeply burnt skin.

"You didn't have this on the earthen plane." Alastor pressed the point of his knife against the raised skin. "I would have noticed."

"Don't." Shay's eyes were wide, remembering how Chel and Jed had held her down and tried to cut it open. "Please. Just leave it alone. Haven't you done enough to me today?"

Alastor rubbed his thumb absently over the scar on her thigh as he stared at her face. "Someone hurt you here, didn't they?"

"You did."

A nauseating smile spread across Alastor's lips. "I'll do more," he promised.

Shay felt sick. Bile rose in the back of her throat. She squeezed her eyes shut and tried to ignore the twisting sensation in her stomach. "Don't touch me. Please, just stop."

Her head hurt and her stomach hurt. It felt like she

was being stabbed. Shay screamed as the pain in her stomach tightened and pulled. It yanked once, twice, three times and...

Shay disappeared.

Alastor's hand thumped against the table in the absence of Shay's thigh.

"Interesting," Alastor said as he touched the leather straps which once held her in place.

Alastor crossed the hovel to return the knife to the chopping block in the kitchen. Then he made himself a sandwich and waited for her to come back.

Twenty-Six

THE STRANGE THING about riding a Demon horse is that they might be called for a Crossroads deal at any time. Jed learned this the hard way. One moment he was riding like the devil, wind chapping his face and the next he was on the ground with road rash to his ass.

"Fuck," Jed shouted as he rolled.

Chel's giant boots landed heavy on the crumbling asphalt. He was bent over in laughter, gripping his knees. "You should have seen your sorry hide tumbling down the road."

Jed groaned as he made it to his feet and checked his bag to make sure nothing fell out. He whispered a spell that fixed his torn pants.

"Guess we're walking again." Chel held out his hands. "Or I can take you to the sky." He winked.

"Never," Jed sneered as he secured his pack and headed toward a dirt road. "Just, stop asking."

They had been traveling on foot for half the day when a pub became visible in the distance. Shrouded by long-limbed pine trees, and pushed back from the dirt path they were following, Jed was eager to find a place to rest for a few minutes. Chel was eager to test the alliance of the lesser Demons of Hell.

"Let's see if they know anything." Chel motioned toward the pub. "It will give us a better idea of how many of Alastor's friends we'll be up against when we find him." Chel cracked his knuckles. "Ready to pick a fight?"

"I could kill something." Jed followed the Hellion.

They entered the squat establishment and the chatter of Hellspeak stopped. Only their footsteps were heard as Chel and Jed crossed the room to the seating area of the bar.

There were strange Demons everywhere, creatures like Jed had never seen in his life–only in books. And then some he'd never seen even in the books of the Peabody Library. The one behind the bar was squat and wide, his skin the color of pea soup.

Chel approached the bartender. "I'm looking for a Demon."

"Got plenty of 'em." The bartender waved his hand motioning to the full tables.

"A specific one. He might have been traveling with a human." Chel gripped his Hellion blade just in case anyone needed clarification of what he was.

The bartender's eyes flashed up from cleaning a mug. "You're traveling with a human."

"Not quite." Jed clicked his tongue as he sat and waved extra friendly at a Demon that resembled a bat– just the face, no wings. "Only half human." He winked.

The bat-faced Demon's eyes went wide before his face twisted in disgust.

"Don't toy with the locals," Chel warned Jed under his breath before turning back to the bartender. "His name is Alastor. We have it on good intel that he crossed through these parts."

The bartender's gaze spanned his patrons. The air was heavy with unspoken words. Seemed everyone had something to say but no one was saying it.

"Two ale and bread and cheese." Chel ordered.

"I'll say, Alastor is a right snake." Jed spit on the ground. No one moved.

"That's not quite an insult here." Chel's voice was hushed. "You need to channel something a bit different."

Jed winked. "Hope we find that fluffy unicorn."

"More archaic," Chel whispered.

"Ah right," Jed had to channel ancient books he'd read at Peabody Library, "sheep-biting clotpole."

Three Demons shoved their chairs back and stood.

"There ya go." Chel took a swig of his ale. "Think it was involving the sheep that did it."

Jed's fingertips tingled with magic.

Chel pulled his blade; it hummed to life and glowed.

The bartender scraped a dish across the counter and set down two mugs, the ale sloshing.

Chel reached over and took a mug, sipping from it gently before downing the entire thing in one gulp.

Jed sat and broke the bread. He ate leisurely as Chel fought with the three Demons who had stood. Every so often he'd send a blast of power and knock someone over.

By the time Chel was done fighting, half the pub was empty and Jed had eaten most of the bread and cheese.

"Now," Chel turned to the bartender, "tell me about Alastor."

"He hasn't been around for decades," the bartender said. "Just showed up a few weeks ago and rumor has it he was carrying a woman back to his hovel. She looked human."

"What color was her hair?" Chel asked.

"Blue," the bartender replied.

Chel left coins on the bar to pay for their food.

"Do you need directions to his hovel?" the bartender asked.

"Already know where it is," Jed said as they left.

The surrounding forest was quiet as Jed and Chel made their way to the mountain path.

"There is little allegiance," Chel said.

"You gained that from one bar fight?" Jed asked.

"Most of the Demons left, that tells me all I need to know." Chel looked toward Jed. "And what in the heck is a clotpole?"

Jed shrugged. "Don't know. Read it in a book once."

TWENTY-SEVEN

SHAY HAD NEVER BEEN HAPPIER to see Nero or to be on the Earthen plane and out of that hovel in Hell. She just wished she had some clothes. Nero's head jerked up, blocking her nakedness from the man who'd called them to the crossroads. He looked hopeful and guilty. Typical.

Shay's eyes narrowed on the man. "Give me your shirt."

He leaned to the side and his eyes went straight to her naked breasts.

"Now!" Shay shouted.

The man startled and started unbuttoning his shirt. He tossed it to her.

Shay put the shirt on and refocused on the man as she was doing the buttons. Thankfully the guy was tall and the shirt went well below her hips. She hissed as the fabric touched the burn. She had hoped to find underwear or pants but decided she wasn't going to be able to deal with the rubbing on her hip.

"What do you want?" Shay snapped with the tilt of her head.

There was something warm coming down the tether from Nero. Soothing. Calming. Shay didn't know how all of this worked, she'd narrowly escaped Alastor cutting her open and she needed to figure out a way to escape him.

"I need to make a deal," the shirtless man said.

Shay was calming. As long as she was here, making this deal, she was free. Her fingers tangled in Nero's mane.

"You want someone dead?" Shay asked. "It's always the same with you."

"No," the man corrected. "I'll do the killing. I want immortality."

Nero's ears twitched. He wasn't so sure immortality was a deal they could make. Shay waited for a sign from Nero.

Nero shook his head and huffed.

"Can't do it," Shay said. "No deal."

The shirtless man crossed his arms. Shay noticed the tattoos that ran down his shoulders and across his neck. He looked like a biker or a gang member or someone who did bad deeds.

"I want my wife gone," he finally said.

The images came to Shay–memories of his life, the past, the future, and the woman he wanted gone. There were children. Of course, always children involved. Men rarely considered what the loss of a mother would do to the children. But judging from this man, he didn't care.

Nero nodded in agreement with the pact.

"Your deal is accepted. Out of the eater will come something to eat. And out of the strong will come something sweet." The gold jewelry shined as the deal was accepted.

Nero walked out of the trapping runes that were drawn in the crossroads.

The man's eyes widened. "You're doing it now?"

"Of course," Shay replied.

"Can you give me time to say goodbye?" he asked.

"It doesn't work like that." Shay shook her head. "We have places to go, deals to be made. It happens now."

———

The job was done.

Shay shook leaves from her leg and she gazed at their work. She hated this.

"Nero," Shay's voice was low, "let's run fast."

Nero whinnied, high stepped a few times, then took off.

Shay's skin tingled. Her spine arched as she pressed herself into the wind and held her arms wide. She didn't care about falling off. She knew Nero would never knock her down but she also would do anything to not return to Alastor.

Nero ran faster. They passed cities and towns, valleys, and streams. Nero finally stopped at the lake in the mountain valley, where they'd stopped before. Spring flowers had erupted from the soil, their petals closed to the moonlight.

Shadows moved. It was too familiar for Shay to ignore.

"Are you following me?" Shay snapped.

"It's that hair. Draws me like a moth to a flame." Sparrow gazed at her lazily from under a large oak tree. "I heard a rumor."

"I bet." Shay got off Nero's back, limped when pain sprung from her hip.

"Heard you'd been kidnapped, but here you are. Free as a bird. Killing and making deals on the Earthen plane." His eyes focused on her limp.

Shay held on to Nero for support, unable to put full weight on her leg.

"What do you want, Raven King?" Shay snapped.

"Show me." He motioned to her hip.

"Why?"

"I want to help."

Shay snickered. "I will not owe a debt to you."

"Have you asked your Queen for help?" One dark brow rose on Sparrow's handsome face.

"She doesn't know. Or at least, I'm not sure if she knows."

"Hm." He pointed, thoughtful with her response. "Show me."

Shay lifted the hem of the man's button-down shirt she was wearing and revealed the brand that Alastor had burned into her body.

Sparrow sank to his haunches to get a good look at the blistering skin in the moonlight. "Looks like it hurts." Sparrow stood, rubbing his chin. "The Demon that took you, is he planning to kill you?"

"Just torture. Eons of torture." Shay shivered with the confession. "We busted up his skin trade ring he had going. Now he wants me to pay for all the money he's lost out on. Jed killed him but it didn't stick." Shay rubbed her face in exhaustion. "He was selling kids and women. He's kidnapped me once already, right before we found you in California."

"Your soul will be worth more than money. Your Queen should know that your soul has been stolen."

"You care about my soul?" Shay asked. "It hasn't been stolen. He simply kidnapped me. He's kidnapped me before. I'll get away. Jed will kill him, again."

"You killed an Angel. The Seven Kingdoms of Heaven will want retribution."

"Wonderful."

"They're waiting. Patiently. A soul like yours is valuable."

"I don't care." Shay exhaled. "Also, I'm not dead. My soul is mine. None of ya'll get to lay claim to it." Shay was pointing and there was an edge to her voice. She'd had enough with everyone telling her what to do and when to do it. She'd never lived by the rules of Heaven and Hell and she wasn't about to.

Sparrow nodded, a strange look on his face as he backed into the shadows.

Shay felt the tug in her stomach. It was coming. They were done with their deal making and now she was going to be pulled back to Alastor's hovel. She didn't want to go.

"Help me," Shay whispered to Nero, begged, despair in her voice. "I can't go back to that Demon. You saved me before, boy." She was stroking his cheek. "I need you to find me. I can't go back to him. Alastor is going to torture me."

Sparrow had never left the shadows he'd backed into. He heard Shay's every word. The pain in her voice. Sparrow lacked compassion for most, but Shay didn't deserve this. She'd helped him once. Before he could think longer on the situation, he returned to Heaven in a flash.

TWENTY-EIGHT

SHAY LANDED on her hip when she appeared in Alastor's hovel and her knees gave out from the shock of it all. She cried out in pain, wishing she'd had the forethought to land differently. She hissed and rolled to her stomach, scrambling to stand. Shay got to her knees before a hand was tangling in her hair, pulling her up.

"I've missed you," Alastor said as he pulled her to stand. "What's this?" His hand gripped the collar of her shirt and pulled until two of the buttons popped off.

"You want me naked on the Earthen plane? Imagine what the men there would do." Shay glared at Alastor. She could feel his hot breath on her face as she stared into his dark eyes.

Shay knew she needed to do something different. She wasn't going to be a victim in this. She was stronger and

Chel had taught her to fight. Shay needed to manipulate him just like she'd done that night in the dive bar where she'd met Clyburn.

"You used to be nicer to me," Shay reminded Alastor. "At that camp. You made those men stop trying to hurt me. You made me dinner." She searched his eyes and relaxed her face, tried her best to play the innocent fawn.

Alastor stilled as he stared down at her. "And then you burned down my camp and tried to kill me." He shoved her away.

Shay stumbled over a chair that was behind her but was able to stay upright. She glanced toward the door, wondering if she could beat him to it.

"Sit down," he warned. "Don't even think about it. This is your home now. I've marked you, you're mine. You will always re-appear where I am."

Shay's hip burned as he spoke.

"Where were you? Humans can't disappear like that." He sniffed the air. "You smell like the Earthen plane. Like blood and hate." His eyes glimmered with hope that she'd turned just as dark as him since she'd found her home in Hell.

"I follow the Crossroads Demon. I don't know how or why. It just started happening. I can't control it." Shay winced as Alastor threatened to move closer.

Alastor lay his large hands on the table and pointed. "You go to do Crossroads Demon work, then you come back to me." He jabbed the aged table with this index finger. "There's nothing else." He stood to his full height. "Do you understand? Don't linger."

Shay's heart was beating against her ribs. She didn't want to be scared but Alastor was like a drill Sargent and she didn't want to wind up dead by his hands. She glanced at the door one last time and let all of her hope of escape flutter away.

"I understand," Shay said.

———

WEEKS PASSED and Shay wondered why no one had come to find her. Maybe they'd all decided she wasn't worth saving. She knew she'd upset everyone with sneaking out and refusing to let them cut open her scar. But leaving her at the mercy of a Demon was cruel. She tried to stay strong but the fact that she was alone was tearing her apart.

Alastor always walked the line of barely hospitable and hostile. Sometimes he left for days at a time, returning tired and grumpy. Other days he puttered around the hovel, in and out of his office, making phone calls and dealing deals. He reminded her of a businessman. But then, Alastor *was* a business man. He'd run a human trafficking business between realms for ages. Shay watched him and eavesdropped on every conversation as she did the chores he demanded. Sometimes he simply wanted her to sit and stare, unmoving like a statue. She was bored to tears on those days.

Alastor had given her a room. There was no door and it was across the hall from his, but she had a small bed and a shelf for clothing. He allowed her to shower and eat what she wanted. It was a very confounding situation. He'd threatened her with a lifetime of pain yet treated her like a houseguest most days.

There were nights when he'd come home raging like the Demon that he was. He'd slam doors and punch walls. He'd threaten her, grab at her skin, and promise to do terrible things to her. Shay fought back. She always did. She was puny next to him but she wasn't going to go down without a fight.

"What are you going to do, feeble human?" Alastor's voice was thick with contempt. "I should rip you to shreds."

"What a waste of risking your life to find me then." Shay smirked.

He slapped the scarred brand on her hip and she cried out, scrambling away from him. "I didn't risk shit. That was the simplest task I ever experienced. Getting into the castle was nothing. The Queen of Hell is *weak*. Lucifer would have never allowed that to happen."

She was tempted to stand up for Meg. To tell Alastor that Meg was pregnant, not weak. But Shay was smarter than that. She kept her mouth shut. "You're a fucking bastard," she spat back.

"You have barely broken the surface of what I am." Alastor jabbed a finger to his chest. "You know nothing."

Shay had scratched herself on the table as she scrambled to get away from him and her arm began to bleed.

Alastor's eyes zeroed in on the small drip sliding down her arm. He picked up a chair and slammed it over the table. "Get out of my face and clean yourself," he shouted, throwing the splintered pieces of chair at her.

He didn't have to tell her twice. Shay ran to the bathroom and locked herself inside. She pressed a cloth to her arm until the bleeding stopped, wondering why it had caused such a visceral reaction from him. Then Shay remembered the Hellions who'd come after her for her blood, the way Skeele and Queen Meg acted around each other's blood, and the Hellions drinking from glasses of blood. All these weeks she'd been trapped with him he never took her blood, but always avoided it.

Shay showered then went to her room. The hovel was quiet. Either Alastor had found something to occupy his time or he'd left. Or maybe he was asleep. She took it as time to prepare. Shay dressed then began her nightly exercises. She wasn't going to be weakened by being locked up in this place. She did sit-ups until her stomach ached, pushups until her arms felt like jelly, and lunges until her thighs burned. She'd done this nearly every night, readying herself.

Later, as she lay in bed, thinking about ways to escape, the twinge of pain started in her belly. It was familiar now. Shay sat up and put on her boots. She'd been sleeping fully clothed since Alastor allowed her clothing again. She didn't want any surprises being half dressed. The pain in her stomach intensified; pulled once, twice, three times. Shay disappeared, drawn to whatever crossroads pact was calling her. She smiled inwardly at the thought of seeing Nero again.

TWENTY-NINE

J ED WAS STARTING to feel the fatigue of walking through Hellscape. He glanced up at Chel only to find the Hellion lowering himself to the ground and walking next to Jed, wings tucked tightly against his back.

"We can stop to rest," Chel suggested.

"I can't leave Shay alone with that scum any longer than necessary." Jed noticed he was breathing heavy–it felt like a boulder was crushing him from above.

"If Nero is on Crossroads Demon work, then Shay is with him," Chel reminded. "We have time until Nero returns."

Jed's face twisted. "Something is not right. He's been gone too long. Would a Crossroads Demon be called away for this long?"

The air felt thick. The gravity of Hell pressed down

on his bones. The ochre sun lingered in the sky for an obtrusive amount of time.

Jed paused, rested his hand against a tree trunk. He wiped sweat from his brow. How much time had passed? He wasn't sure. Everything looked familiar and different.

"Have we been here before?" Jed asked.

Chel walked in a tight circle and rubbed his head. "It does look familiar."

Jed crouched and inspected the path just like the Crow men had done. He scanned the ground. "There are no footprints ahead. Old ones behind." He focused, realized their old footprints had filled with dirt and leaves as though days had passed and they hadn't just walked there. "Look," he motioned to Chel.

"Fucking A." Chel pulled his blade, ready to fight.

"Who are you going after?" Jed asked.

"Those bastards at the pub. It was them. I know it."

Static sparked from Jed's fingertips. "Let me try something." He pulled the notebook from his pocket and searched through it for a moment.

"Have you encountered something like this before?" Jed asked.

"Never." Chel was fuming.

"Heard any rumors about this? Is time repeating? What is this we are stuck in? I think time is moving very slowly."

Chel paced, thinking. His arm brushed against a tree, dust fell. Chel stopped moving and felt stiffness in his joints. "It's…"

Chel remained still, slowed his breathing. Dust collected on his shoulders and shoes. He looked up at Jed who was deep in thought reading spells, searching for something to help them out of this, now covered in a layer of white dust. It fluttered away from the pages as he turned them.

"I know of this. It's a potion to slow us. Walking slower and slower on the same path." Chel replaced his blade. "Even if we get back to the pub, much time will have passed." He wiped the white dust off his arm. "We must keep moving before we turn to stone. We must return to the pub and destroy the mother potion."

"How long have we been like this?" Jed tucked his notebook in a pocket.

"If the dust is settling on us, too long. Days. Maybe longer."

The men walked, eager to move, and they noticed that the shadows passing over them were not a bird in the sky but the coming and going of night. They took five footsteps and two nights came and went, maybe longer. It was hard to discern in the state they were in. So much could be missed in a blink.

"I must get to Shay." Jed walked faster but the

potion worked in a way that made him continue to move slow. It was a slow rot concoction, one that caused the men to dwindle and wane. It wanted him to stop and rest and turn to stone and decay under the ochre Hell-sky. They would never make it back to the pub. It was impossible. They'd be moss covered stone before they got there; joints arthritic and unmoving, minds slowed to molasses. And so, the rescuers needed their own saving.

THIRTY

AT THE CROSSROADS

SPARROW DREW a rune in the dirt and called upon the Crossroads Demon. He shouldn't have meddled, especially since he despised others meddling. It was a task usually reserved for the Deacons but they seemed to have turned a blind eye to the situation. Sparrow crossed his arms and flexed his wings. He shouldn't have had them visible on the Earthen plane, but he was standing in the middle of nowhere and the night breeze felt heavenly between his feathers. He tipped his neck to the side just so until it cracked. He needed more time away. Rebuilding his kingdom was a giant pain in the ass. After the Fast-Zombie War and the Basilisk visit, he barely had any of his own people. Sparrow took his father's throne only to be designated the weakest in the Seven Kingdoms of Heaven. It was embarrassing but utterly no fault of his own. He simply needed to build it up. There were plenty of souls to go around.

His thoughts went to the Demon who had taken Shay. Sparrow could work with that creature to secure souls. Kings before him had done it. No one rose to power without doing some dastardly deeds. No one was pure. Sparrow certainly wasn't. His angelic wholesomeness had been burned out of him by curses and lies and deception.

Nero and Shay arrived with a *crack* and walked closer, confined to the circle of runes he'd drawn.

"I want to make a deal." The night breeze disrupted the way the black feathers laid at the arch of his wings. It made him look disheveled.

"It seems kinda wrong. You're an Angel. A King. Aren't there rules against making deals with Demons?"

Sparrow shrugged. "I don't really care. You're not really a Demon." His eyes narrowed as he noticed her torn clothing, more marks on her arms and legs, and her bandaged arm with drying blood. Sparrow's mouth watered. He swallowed the urge back. "Your boyfriend hasn't found you yet?"

Shay bit her lip, held back tears. She'd cried enough

for Jed to find her. But it had been weeks. Something happened to him. She figured he was probably dead. Or he left her. She had never felt more alone.

Shay tipped her chin up. "I don't know where he is."

"That's too bad. I heard a rumor that he's missing." Sparrow's features were impassive.

Tears welled behind Shay's eyes but she refused to let them fall. Daddy raised her to be stronger than this. She was a cowgirl through and through. Daddy taught her to survive the apocalypse if she were all alone; this was nothing. Shay rotated her shoulders and straightened her back.

"You hear a lot of rumors. Now. What do you want?" Shay asked.

Nero whinnied and bobbed his head in agreement.

"A deal against a Demon," Sparrow said.

"We need more details than that."

"Against a Demon who deals in flesh." Sparrow cocked an eyebrow.

"Be more specific."

Sparrow sat in the thick grass and motioned across from him. "Sit with me. Negotiate."

"I don't have time for this." Shay shivered, feeling a chill pass under her skin. She and Nero were getting annoyed with the lack of details.

"You want time for this. Negotiation. Every moment you are here with me, you are not with your captor."

"How heroic of you," Shay said as she swung her leg and climbed down from Nero's back. "I guess this torture is better than the alternative." Shay sat at the edge of the circular rune. Nero lay next to her, facing Sparrow. "Negotiate." She waved her arms open in anticipation like she was accepting a hug from a friend.

Sparrow tapped his chin. "A deal against a Demon who deals in flesh." He paused again, toying.

"I only know of one at the moment."

"You might meet more, soon. If I make a deal with a Crossroads Demon, what will you take from me?" Sparrow asked.

"It is unknown," Shay replied as Nero watched the conversation closely. "Out of the eater will come something to eat. And out of the strong will come something sweet." Shay sighed. "You will be eaten."

Sparrow made a face that indicated the threat didn't sound too terrible and perhaps he'd received worse threats. "To be eaten doesn't mean I must die."

"I don't make the rules, I just live by them." Shay reached to the side and patted Nero absently. "But the others, they have only made a one sided deal, they didn't negotiate for what we would take."

"Their loss," Sparrow said with a smirk. "You can consume something else from me."

"Possibly," Shay said.

"You know, most of these deals you make are simply a transfer of souls. One soul for another. There is balance in the Crossroads deal."

Shay nodded. "It's true."

Sparrow smiled, brought out all the charm until he saw the hitch in her breath. He could indulge, mar her morals, and draw her away from Jed. It would be easy to seduce her. It always was easy to seduce humans. Sparrow released a breath. No, he liked her and that shade of blue hair, but Shay was not his type. Her hair wasn't black, her skin not covered in ink, there was no scar over her heart, and he didn't have the burning desire to stab her so she'd be consumed with revenge and obsessed with him. No, he wouldn't try and seduce her. Shay was someone he needed on his side. She'd have to learn how to walk the tightrope and balance her loyalty to the Queen of Hell and the Raven King.

Shay's soul was the equivalent of diamonds and rubies and piles of gold, and Sparrow was going to find a way to make it his.

THIRTY-ONE

"Put this on," Alastor said as he stood in the doorway to Shay's room. He tossed a bag on the floor and checked his watch. "We are leaving in one hour."

"We?" Shay's throat felt dry. She hadn't left the hovel except to go on Crossroads Demon missions. Alastor hadn't been happy that she was gone so long on the last Crossroads deal. It was a gift from the Raven King. One she'd never mention to Alastor. She wasn't sure why Sparrow was so interested in her all of a sudden.

"Get ready." Alastor turned on his heel, crossed the hallway to his room, and closed the door.

Shay moved from the bed and opened the bag. There was a dress inside. She brought it to the bathroom, showered, and slipped the garment on.

The dress was black with rhinestones and had a slit

up the thigh, all the way to her hip, showing the rune Alastor had branded her with. She wished she could twist up her hair but she had nothing here. Shay stared at herself in the mirror. In a dress like this, she wasn't sure what to expect. She wished she had makeup. No, change that. She was glad she didn't have makeup. She should rub dirt on her body and wreck her hair and make herself look like a pig in a dress. Whatever Alastor was up to, she didn't want to participate willingly.

Shay opened the bathroom door. Alastor was standing there in a black suit. Waiting.

Shay held her breath and stepped to the side. "Why am I wearing this?" she asked.

"We have a party to attend." Alastor waved her toward the door.

"I don't have any shoes."

"You won't need them."

Shay swallowed hard and her mind traveled at warp speed, imagining scenarios. The split in her dress showed a lot of leg as she walked quickly to keep up with Alastor. She stepped past the threshold to the hovel and paused, taking a deep breath. She had nearly forgotten how the ochre sky glowed, how everything looked so shadowed.

"Come on," Alastor ordered as he walked toward a Jeep.

"You have a car?" Shay asked.

Alastor opened the passenger door and waited. "Most inhabitants of Hell do. We aren't so uncultured, human." He glanced down at her. "I borrowed it." His tone was clipped.

Shay got in the passenger seat and Alastor shoved the door closed before walking around the Jeep and getting in the driver seat.

Shay rubbed her feet on the floor mat, cleaning them of dirt from the walk to the Jeep.

Alastor drove crumbling roads through the mountain. Everything looked unfamiliar yet vaguely familiar. Shay had been told that Hell was nothing more than a dark reflection of the Earthen plane. Maybe she'd been through these mountains before. Shay worried at what awaited her. She never hoped for the Crossroads pact to call her away, but tonight she did. She didn't want to face whatever Alastor had planned.

Shay fidgeted with a rhinestone on her dress and shifted in her seat to relieve the pressure off her branded hip. It ached. She glanced at Alastor. He was focused on the road, the shadows of his face churning as though he were deep in thought. Shay recognized it as the mask of a man preparing to make deals. He warned she'd repay him.

Shay glanced out the window. She wanted to run. She didn't want to repay him with her flesh. Sadness flooded her chest as she thought about Jed and why he hadn't come to find her.

Alastor turned down a long driveway that ended at a black mansion pressed into the forest. There were other vehicles and a steady stream of Demons and strange creatures walking inside. He parked the Jeep and got out.

Alastor opened the passenger side door and waited.

Shay didn't move.

"Get out," he warned.

She shook her head.

Alastor snapped his fingers and the brand on her hip burned like it was new again.

Vehicles filled the parking area. People—no, Demons—walked to the grand front entrance dressed in suits and dresses. Although, Shay noticed, she saw more suits than dresses and wondered why. She'd seen very few Demon females in her time.

The Demon party resembled a gathering of the rich and famous on the Earthen plane, Shay supposed, since she'd never been to a party like that before; she had only seen them on TV and in the movies.

Small creatures carried trays with champagne and food. She tried not to stare at the Demons of all shapes and sizes. Horns and leathered skin met formal suits and dresses. Many turned to watch when Alastor entered with Shay following close behind.

Shay looked down at her bare feet and felt under-dressed.

There was conversation, but it sounded strange to Shay's ears. Hellspeak. They were conversing in Hellspeak, a completely different language. She wouldn't have a clue what they were discussing. Shay watched Alastor's facial features to try and guess what he was saying as he greeted a tall Demon with goat-like horns and a white beard. The Demon scrutinized her, an eerie smile on his face. Their Hellspeak sounded garbled and wicked. Goat horns licked his lips with a split tongue.

A shiver tore down Shay's spine. They were watching her, judging. Some walked around her like she was cattle ripe for bidding.

She closed her eyes and wished for that sharp feeling in her gut to pull her away.

It never came.

Someone touched her arm. Shay glanced from the corner of her eye and saw a black nail dragging down her skin. She looked up to a giant Demon with black horns and black claws. He wore a suit with diamond studded lapels.

"We match, don't you think?" the Demon said in English.

"I don't think so," Shay replied, taking a step away, toward Alastor.

A warm arm wrapped around Shay's waist and held on tight.

Alastor said something to the Demon with the diamond lapels that sounded like a joking threat. He squeezed Shay against him.

Shay went stiff. She didn't want Alastor's hands on her. She glanced at the door. Alastor pressed her against him again and sipped at his champagne.

———

The party went on entirely too long in Shay's opinion. She was glad to be away from the leering gazes and strange fingers stroking her arms like they were testing the thickness of her skin.

"Thank you for finally leaving," Shay said sarcastically as Alastor opened the door to the Jeep.

"I should have stayed. We were taking preliminary bids," Alastor replied.

"On what?"

"You." He smirked darkly. "You're going to help me get the skin trades up and running again. Remember?"

Shay sighed and leaned against the car door. She had to find a way to escape before something terrible happened to her. She needed to escape and find Jed. She was sure no one else would look for him. He'd spend most of his life as a loner; it seemed he never created lasting friendships with anyone. Shay figured that was why their relationship was so touch and go.

"Stop thinking of him," Alastor warned. "You are mine now."

"I don't belong to anyone."

Alastor snapped his fingers and the brand burned.

Shay hissed in pain. "Fine. Ok. Whatever."

Alastor was smirking as he drove, like he had a secret. Like he knew everything.

"What?" Shay demanded.

"I paid some friends to poison them." He checked his watch like he was late for a date. "They're probably turned to stone by now. It's been long enough."

Shay's worse fear had come true. Jed was probably dead and it was Alastor's doing. "You are a fucking bastard," she seethed with all the venom she could muster.

THIRTY-TWO

AT THE CROSSROADS

"WHAT'S WRONG, BOY?" Shay asked as she absently rubbed circles on Nero's shoulder.

He turned his head to look at her, his eyes glassy.

"Are you sad?" Shay asked. "I'm sad too." She leaned forward to lay across his neck. "I'm so lonely and scared."

Nero whinnied something forlorn and gnashed his teeth together. He sent emotion down the tether that bound them, hoping she might understand why he hadn't attempted to save her yet. It was too dangerous; they'd die without Jed and the Hellion.

Shay stilled for a moment as she processed.

"Have you been searching for Jed?"

Nero wagged his head in a yes motion.

"Stop looking," Shay warned. "He's dead. Alastor had him poisoned. Said he's turned to stone. It's just me and you now."

Nero looked away. Although the sound of having Shay to himself was exquisite, he knew it wasn't right. They both needed Jed to make it through this. Nero pawed the ground with a front hoof. He wasn't so sure Jed was gone.

At the desolate crossroads where the boundary between the mortal realm and the abysmal depths blurred, Shay was caught between two worlds, her presence a haunting reminder of the fragile balance between light and darkness.

The air crackled with an ominous energy as the figure approached the crossroads, their steps hesitant yet filled with a sense of desperate determination. They bore the weight of something heavy upon their shoulders, their gaze haunted by the specter of tragedy that loomed over their existence.

It was a Deacon.

Nero backed up.

Shay tensed.

Deacons were the gatekeepers of balance between the

Seven Kingdoms of Heaven, the Earthen plane, and Hell. Why did one summon Shay and Nero?

"What is it that you seek, Deacon?" Shay asked.

The Deacon hesitated, their gaze flickering with uncertainty before they spoke, voice tinged with a mixture of power and desperation.

"No one can know that I'm here," the Deacon said.

Shay nodded. "Is that your deal?"

"No." the Deacon folded his hands. "This deal will be a great burden for both of us."

The Deacon kept looking over his shoulder and to the desert beyond. He'd drawn them to a crossroads in the middle of nowhere. They could see for miles even with only moonlight.

"There is a great darkness coming," the Deacon warned.

"That sounds like a warning, not a deal. Why did you call me here?" Shay didn't want to return to Alastor but she didn't want her time wasted by this creature.

The Deacon paused and closed his eyes, finding calm and choosing his words carefully. "The deal is, you must take the children to safety and tell no one where they are. You must hide them until Clea's prophecy comes to fruition."

"What children?"

The Deacon held up a finger. "They are not born

yet. When the time comes, you will know. You must agree to this now, before it's too late."

"What are you wishing to give me?" Shay asked, knowing that what the Crossroads Demon would take was not negotiable and typically unknown.

"I will give my life. Sooner rather than later."

Shay searched his face. He was so plain there was no way she'd be able to tell who he was, but that was the way of the Deacons. They looked the same, sounded the same. They could blend into a crowd and never be seen again. Once he left, Shay knew they'd have a hard time finding him again.

The rings on Nero's ear and Shay's hand shimmered with agreement.

Shay held out her hand and the Deacon reached forward to shake on the deal.

"Why here?" Shay asked. "Why not come to me in Hell?"

"This is God's land," the Deacon said. "I needed witness that I tried to prevent what was coming. God must know we tried." His hands shook.

Shay wasn't sure why she'd become the resident babysitter in Hell. First Thrush and now this. But she wouldn't let children suffer; couldn't.

The Deacon nodded then backed away. There was no portal in the desert, no water, nothing. The Deacon just walked away across the sand until his figure wavered like a mirage and eventually disappeared.

"Whatever that was all about, I hope you're there to help me." Shay rubbed Nero's neck.

He huffed and scraped his hoof over the markings on the ground, releasing them. Shay was grateful she didn't have to kill anyone tonight.

"Run, boy," Shay whispered.

Nero took off, only stopping when he reached their valley.

Sparrow didn't appear from the shadows near the valley like before. There was only the hushed lapping of lake water, the gentle song of crickets, the warm summer breeze. Perhaps the Deacon scared him off?

"I don't want to go back," Shay said to Nero, rubbing her cheek against his neck.

The brand on her hip didn't listen. She returned to the hovel with a sickening feeling in her gut that had nothing to do with the travel from the Earthen plane to Hell.

THIRTY-THREE

Alastor was waiting, dressed in a black suit, hair styled, and smelling like fresh brimstone.

"Put this on," Alastor said as he tossed Shay a garment. This was becoming too familiar. Twice now: the same motion, the same orders.

Shay rubbed thin fabric between her fingertips. She started to make her way to the bathroom.

"No," Alastor said, "here, now. Put it on. We're late."

Shay didn't want to get naked in front of the Demon. He'd seen everything she had to offer before but it was a precarious position to be in. She took off her shirt, dropped it to the floor and pulled the garment over her head. It was another dress, this one shorter than before; silver, and with another slit up the hip. She shimmied her pants off and stood with her spine straight for Alastor's inspection, the scar on her thigh visible for all to see.

Alastor circled her. He was too close, his breath sifting across her skin. He had a knife, always carried one now. Something old. He pressed it against the scar on her thigh.

"We still haven't talked about this."

"Leave it alone." Shay met his gaze. "Please," she said through gritted teeth as memories of people she'd considered friends held her down to cut it open.

"My associates are going to want answers. They don't want skin with ugly scars like this." He pressed the tip of the knife to the jagged disfigurement. "I should cut it off."

He was too close and probably heard Shay swallow hard at the mention of what he'd like to do.

"Your *associates* should be happy with what they get." Shay's skin felt tight and she wanted nothing more than to go to sleep after crying on Nero's shoulder for the past hour.

"They bring the money to help pay off your debt. I'll bring them what they wish." Alastor removed the knife tip from her skin and secured the blade under his suit jacket. "Let's go."

As much of a bastard as Alastor was, he held the

door for her as they exited the hovel. He opened the passenger door of the Jeep and waited for her to sit before closing it. He treated her as equal parts something precious and something despised.

Alastor took the same route to the black mansion in the woods. They were much later than last time, the only ones crossing the parking pad and walking to the giant glass door.

All heads turned when Alastor entered and stepped to the side. Some Demons licked their lips, nearly all stared. Shay felt naked in the thin, revealing dress.

Alastor led Shay down a hallway with a winding stairwell with black marble and deep red carpet. He stopped in what looked like a dining room with three pedestals. Two women were standing on the pedestals, each wearing a dress similar to Shay's. They had shoes.

"Get up there," Alastor ordered.

Shay walked, silently in her bare feet, and stepped up onto the pedestal in the middle. She met the gazes of the other women. They were young, beautiful and... human.

A sickening feeling tore at Shay's stomach as Alastor walked closer, looking like the predator that he was.

"What are you doing?" Shay asked. "Humans aren't supposed to be in this realm."

"But look at you here. Now, shut up." Alastor walked around the other women first, inspecting and nodding approval. "These ladies might be able to teach you a few things about being on display for the bidders."

Neither said a word; they both faced forward, dead-eyed grins on their faces when Alastor tested their resilience by touching their skin, their hair, their breasts. He licked their shoulders and smelled them loudly.

Shay shivered, disgusted.

"Don't do that, Shay," Alastor warned. "Be still, like these ones." There was a knock on the door to the room. "Be grateful that you're alive and I don't let these Demons do what they want." Alastor flashed a fiery gaze before he went and opened the door. "You are a delicacy to them. They'd eat you whole."

The Demons entered the room, taking seats in the chairs surrounding the pedestals.

Shay realized what was happening. This was an auction. She swallowed hard and tipped her chin up. She focused on the wall in the distance and did her best to hide her fear. She was looking for an escape but soon realized she'd never get out of this room with all the Demons that filled it.

Garbled speech echoed in her ears as the Demons chatted in Hellspeak.

Shay closed her eyes, only opening them again when she heard Alastor's voice. He started auctioning off the girl on the left first. Hands rose, money was promised.

Shay watched the girl pose demurely, making eye contact with the Demons raising flags and the ones who'd placed bets prior. She was edging them to pay more and more until it was finally over. Something similar happened to the girl on her right. Flags raised in eager bidding. The girl posed like a model for a fashion shoot, engaging the crowd.

And then it was Shay's turn. Alastor was standing close, touching her hair and making comments that she couldn't understand. Alastor's hand reached for her face, his index finger and thumb forcing her lips into a smile.

The crowd laughed.

Shay forced a smile and froze her chin to stop it from quivering. Too many flags were raised. Alastor was talking fast in their language. She didn't know what the garbled speech meant, but there was a joking tone and laughter from the crowd as he clearly said things about her.

Someone pointed to Shay's thigh.

Alastor's hand smoothed over her leg, rubbing it. Shay hated that she found his touch comforting, possibly even grounding. She hated him but she knew no one, knew nothing. She told herself that he'd treat her kindly, that he wouldn't let the others hurt her. It was an inner mantra of lies that kept her standing on two feet. She was afraid she'd collapse if she focused on all the terrible things that were going to happen to her. She blinked back a tear and prayed Daddy never got wind of this. He'd be so disappointed to see how far she'd fallen after all he'd taught her to stay alive.

When the auction was over, the Demons filed out of the room. The girls stood, waiting.

Alastor handed glasses of champagne to the other two and dismissed them to a door at the back of the room. He had two glasses of champagne in his hands as he approached Shay.

"Well, the bidding didn't get as high as I would have liked, but it's a good start." He moved the flutes to one hand and reached up, offering his free hand to support Shay as she stepped down from the pedestal.

"Cheers." He handed her champagne.

Shay hesitated, her heart beating wildly against her ribs. She had the slight feeling that she might faint.

"Drink it," Alastor ordered. "It will take the edge off."

The last time Shay had champagne, she was celebrating Meg's release at the castle. That was the night Jed danced with her and kissed her for all to see, claiming her. The sweet smell of the champagne brought it all crashing back. It seemed like forever ago. And now he was dead.

She threw her head back and downed the entire glass in two swallows.

Alastor was sipping at his flute, brows raised. "Should I be impressed or concerned?"

"Fuck right off." Shay threw the flute on the floor and watched it shatter against the marble tiles.

Shay's head felt foggy.

"I expected you to nurse that for a bit. Guess we'll head to the next stop."

Shay stumbled. "What are you talking about?"

Alastor grabbed her upper arm to steady her. "It's time to deliver you to the highest bidder." He checked his watch. "Paid a premium price for five hours. Better get you there before the drugs wear off."

Shay's vision blurred. The bastard had drugged her. She slapped at him as she stumbled to keep up with his pace. Shay tripped once and Alastor lifted her off her feet, carrying her. She could feel the cool air on her ass cheeks as her dress stretched against his arms. But Shay didn't care because her body felt warm and her lower abdomen filled with an ache that she needed to satisfy.

Shay didn't see the Demons watching Alastor carry her out of the black mansion with envy. They licked their lips and touched themselves. They reached for her and Alastor growled like the wild beast he was to keep them at a distance.

He tucked Shay into the passenger seat of the Jeep, buckled her seatbelt, and closed the door.

Her figure was slouched in the front seat as he got behind the wheel and started driving away. He calculated how long the drugs might last, since Shay unexpectedly downed all of them in one swallow. She was supposed to sip demurely, like a lady, so the drugs would enter her system slowly. Alastor glanced at her, the scar on her thigh illumined by moonlight. Her skirt was cinched around her waist, leaving nothing to the imagination. Alastor smirked to himself, glad that he'd arranged the death of her boyfriend. The trash didn't deserve her. Alastor decided, when she was done making him money, he'd keep her. He'd always wanted to. Alastor had caught the change in her demeanor when he'd touched her scarred thigh during the auction. She'd calmed, her heart rate had slowed, she trusted him. Not much but enough to make a difference.

He touched her leg again now as he drove.

Shay startled and mumbled, her foggy mind trying to make sense of where she was.

Shay noticed the hand on her leg and looked up. "How much did you get for me?"

"Not nearly as much as you need to pay your debt to me," Alastor replied with a smirk. "But it's a start."

Shay made a noise deep in her throat.

"Don't worry, he'll be gentle with you." Alastor squeezed Shay's leg and chuckled coldly.

Rage filled Shay's bones. She had nothing left to lose. Shay lurched forward, grabbed the steering wheel, and jerked it to the side as hard as she could.

The Jeep veered off the crumbling mountain road. It rolled, over and over and over as it fell to the ravine below.

THIRTY-FOUR

AT THE CROSSROADS

SHAY NEVER FELT the familiar tug in her gut as she was called to the crossroads. She arrived aching, dirty, covered in blood, and her dress torn. Rolling onto the ground as though she fell from the sky, she stopped abruptly as she hit the edge of the crossroads summoning rune.

"What the fuck happened to you?" Sparrow asked.

"It was a car accident." Shay adjusted her dress.

"Is that blood?" he asked.

"It's not mine," Shay replied as she searched her body for injuries and rolled to sit up.

"That's not reassuring."

"I might have some bruises. Good thing I was wearing my seatbelt." Shay smiled weakly as she leaned against Nero for support.

"Wash that blood off," Sparrow demanded.

"I don't see a nice little bathroom anywhere around here so this is what you get." Shay held her sore arm and thought about sitting down.

"Over there." Sparrow was pointing to the lake.

"I can't leave the circle," Shay reminded him.

"Make a deal with me and leave it." Sparrow smirked.

"Fine. What do you want?" she asked.

Sparrow toyed with the edge of his wings. "I need the feather of a night owl. Just one or two will do."

Shay's eyes narrowed. "What exactly is a *night owl*?"

"It's related to the snowy owl. I'm sure you can figure it out." Sparrow's brow rose. "Are you going to leave the circle?"

"You want the feathers now?" Shay asked.

"Nah, later." It was a riddle she needed to solve, and Sparrow knew it would take time. He wasn't in a rush. He needed time for everything to fall into place.

Nero's ears twitched in agreement and Shay felt the golden ring on her hand surge with excitement.

"Fine." Shay held out a dusky hand with long necrotic fingernails. She shivered as she saw it, something grotesque and cursed. She blinked and her hand returned to normal.

Sparrow didn't seem bothered as he shook on the deal.

"See, that wasn't so hard." Sparrow moved to the side as Shay left the rune circle, Nero close behind her. "Next we work on the big deal." He spread is arms wide. "It's gonna be huge."

"Uh-huh." Shay said absently as she crouched near the lake and washed the blood off her arms with cold water.

Sparrow leaned back, crossing his long legs in front of him and propping himself up with his elbows. He looked too relaxed. But Shay was sure the Raven King didn't have much to fear with the power she could feel radiating off him.

Shay left the pond, Nero close behind her. They settled on the tall grass near Sparrow.

Nero folded his legs to lay down and snacked on the Earthen plane grass, taking special interest in the purple flowers. He closed his eyes as he chewed, savoring the flavor of spring time.

Shay tore long pieces from their roots and began braiding them. Her arms were sore and her ribs ached. Shay wasn't sure how many times the Jeep had rolled after she pulled the wheel. She'd been pulled away before it stopped. She hoped Alastor was dead.

Shay leaned back, her head resting on Nero's flank as he ate.

"Did you call me here just to hang out?" Shay asked.

"We made a deal and we have another deal to discuss."

"Ah, yes, the Demon." Her deft fingers braided another cluster of grass blades.

"I want the Demon." Sparrow's voice was without inflection.

"And my payment?" Shay asked. "Nero's? This is a huge request. Usually people just want someone killed. You're asking for an entire being."

Something sparked in her mind. Jed.

"Ask," Sparrow replied.

"Jed is dead. Alastor had him killed."

Sparrow frowned. "Are you sure?"

"When a Demon such as Alastor tells me he paid his little Demon buddies to kill my boyfriend, I believe him."

"But do you believe that Jed's actually dead?"

Shay shrugged and swallowed back tears.

"You love him?" Sparrow asked.

"I'm mad at him for not doing the right thing so

many times. But yes, I love him. I can forgive him for the things we need to work on together."

Sparrow was silent for a long while before he said, "You know when souls die they go to Meg's plane. They go to a Safe House for sorting or repenting. For deciding where their final resting place will be. Heaven or Hell or the Astral plane."

"So he's still in Hell if he's dead?"

Sparrow cleared his throat. "There's one more piece to the puzzle. Since he's half angel, he could go elsewhere, he could not actually die." Sparrow was watching her. "Did Jed tell you who his father is? That little detail might make a difference."

Shay shook her head. "Do you know?" she asked.

"I don't." Sparrow lay back, threading his fingers behind his head and watching the stars twinkle above them in the night.

"You have power," Shay said. "You can do things, make deals of your own." She sighed. "I need you to find Jed for me. Whatever is left of him."

"I want the Demon to be compelled to follow my every order." Sparrow moved an arm, plucking at the grass.

"You want a Demon slave?" Shay asked. "For how long?"

"Forever."

"And you'll do what I asked?" Shay was wary. She knew better than to trust the Raven King but this was imperative.

"Yes."

Shay looked at Nero and a silent agreement of the proposed deal passed between them. She scooted closer to Sparrow and held out her hand. "Deal."

"Deal." Sparrow shook her hand, his grip harder than before, a shine in his eyes. "One last thing." Sparrow jerked her closer until she could feel his breath on her face. "I find Jed, I get something from you."

Shay's eyes searched his face. She was beginning to realize that deals with the Raven King would never end. She was being pulled into his tangled web and this was probably why Jed had tried to hide her from Sparrow when they were searching for him in California. The Raven King was nothing more than a deadly spider lying in wait. There was so much about Heaven and Hell that Shay didn't know. She was ignorant to the way things worked, but she knew one thing: she loved Jed and she needed to know where he was, she needed to know if he could be brought back like Nightingale. She'd do anything. He was all she had, after all.

"What else do you want?" Shay asked.

"Your soul is mine when you die."

Shay swallowed hard. Nero whinnied behind her

and moved to his feet. He was pawing at the ground and wagging his head.

"Tell your Demon horse to move back," Sparrow warned.

Shay held out her free hand, urging Nero to keep his distance.

"Your soul?" Sparrow repeated.

"Yes."

His grip was too tight, the bones of her fingers rubbed.

"Are you ever going to tell me this Demon's name or do I have to figure that out myself?" Shay asked.

"Alastor." Sparrow smiled.

Thirty-Five

Alastor was bandaging his arm when Shay appeared in the hovel. Just like he'd promised, she always came back to him.

"I should destroy you," he snorted. "You nearly got us fucking killed." His voice was too calm for what she'd done.

Shay said nothing, simply stood still as a statue in her torn dress that was coated in dirt and blood.

"Are you injured?" Alastor asked.

"I didn't think you'd care." Shay's body was sore all over, the deal with Sparrow fresh in her mind.

He was scanning her as he spoke. "I'm not sure you realize how much you've cost me with your little attempt to kill us both." Alastor threw down a rag and stood. "We missed your appointment. I had to make promises that I couldn't afford. I had to make the other girls do double duty." He glanced at his watch. "You've been gone for hours."

Shay shrugged. "When they call at the crossroads, I must go."

"We'll have to fix that."

Shay felt weary after all she'd been through the past evening. She stumbled to the table where Alastor was standing, dragged a chair out and sat.

"I didn't say you could sit," Alastor sneered. "Get up."

Shay took a deep breath. "I literally can't." She held her hand up and showed that it was shaking.

Alastor was fuming as he went to the kitchen and opened the fridge. He slammed the glass on the countertop as he took out orange juice and filled it.

Shay closed her eyes for just a moment, afraid she'd fall asleep and then he'd do something terrible to her. She opened her eyes again as footsteps neared.

Alastor was close. "Drink this."

Shay stared at the glass. She didn't want to drink it, but she was hungry and tired, and she feared what Alastor would do if she disobeyed him again.

Shay slowly sipped at the juice. "You have oranges in Hell?"

"We have more than you know." He waited, standing

entirely too close to her, smelling like a bonfire and whiskey and dried blood.

Shay felt better as the juice settled in her stomach. When she set the glass on the table, Alastor took it away and washed it.

He was standing near the sink, clothing rumpled, hair a mess, looking completely opposite the well-dressed Demon who'd started the night. Alastor's hands gripped the countertop like he was waiting for something.

"What?" Shay asked. "You want to punish me? I'd rather be dead than sold to a Demon. I'd do it again. *I'll do it again.*" She pointed at him. "I can promise…" Shay's tongue felt too big for her mouth and her mind went fuzzy. It was the same way she felt at the black mansion after Alastor had drugged her.

He smiled.

Shay should have known better. She'd never accept food or drink from him again. She kicked the chair back and stood, wobbly on her feet.

"I told you that you'd pay off your debt." He pushed away from the counter. "One way or another."

Shay shook her head to chase away the fog, felt her body go loose. Heat flooded her limbs. That itch in her lower belly ached, begged to be sated.

No. No. Shay tried to tell herself. *It's the drugs. It's not you. It's not him.*

The problem was, she didn't protest as he lifted her. She didn't move her arm as he draped it over his neck.

"I told myself I wouldn't test these goods until after. But since you're so intent on killing yourself and me, I'll do it now, before it's too late." Alastor's voice was smooth as silk, dark as night, sharp as the blade he kept under his suit jacket.

Shay heard the sound of a door being kicked open–her room didn't have a door. They were in his room.

She closed her eyes and tried to right her brain, tried to talk herself awake and into the right mind. Nothing worked. Heat flowed through her veins as the drugs spread.

Alastor settled her on the bed and tugged her body until she lay in the center. He kicked off his fancy shoes and undid his tie, tossing it toward the pillows.

Shay could only watch, groggy, and limbs heavy as cement.

He kicked off his pants, tossed his suit jacket and tore the buttons on his shirt, leaving it open. Alastor was a Demon, but his body was hard and muscled like a bodybuilder; tall but not too bulky. The hollows and planes of his body were on full display.

Shay looked away. She didn't want to see him, didn't want to see what he was going to do to her. She focused on the dark wood of the furniture, the black sheets, the red satin pillows. Anything but him.

The bed dipped as he crawled. She felt his tongue on her ankle. Felt his hand wrap around and tug her leg to the side. A small noise escaped her throat.

Alastor chuckled as he continued to climb up her body. "You're so small," he whispered against her thigh. "Those bastards at the auction would have torn you apart."

"Go away," Shay forced out.

"You smell like the Earthen plane. Like true sunshine. Yellow and crisp." He ran his lips across her unscarred thigh. "Always have. Guess that's what makes you so valuable. You don't smell like Hell. Not entirely at least. Just a little bit right here." He licked her scar. "And here." He grabbed a strand of her long blue hair and tugged.

He reached for her dress and tore it up from the hem. "You've cost me so much money."

Shay fought her muscles, tried to get her legs to move.

"Don't fight me, Shay." His tongue was on her belly, licking upward. "It will be easier this way. You'll understand punishment and behave." He tore her dress further until it was shredded.

Underneath the haze of the drugs, Shay's body was

panicking. She didn't want Alastor to touch her like this. Didn't want to come to the full realization that she was nothing but commercial flesh to the Demons of Hell now.

If she could puke she would.

Alastor grabbed the tie from where he'd thrown it near the pillows. He was straddling her hips and she could see the bulge under his boxers. He took her arm and wrapped the tie around her wrist, forming a loose knot. He slid the tie up her arm and tightened it.

He was reaching for the nightstand. Shay heard the clank of metal and glass. She summoned enough energy to turn her head and watch as he prepared a needle and vial.

"No," Shay forced out.

Alastor sat back, trapping Shay underneath him. He bent, his face too close to hers. Warm breath brushed her neck as his arm pressed across her collarbone. She couldn't move, could barely breathe. He stretched her arm out with the tie, tightened it more, then slapped the crook of her arm.

"There we go." Alastor was whispering something in Hellspeak as the glass clanged.

Then, she felt a pinch and opened her eyes to see red liquid fill the vial. Alastor was taking her blood.

When Alastor pulled the needle out, he was greedy,

pressing his lips to the crook of her arm as it bled, sucking and licking until the puncture wound clotted, leaving a bruise on her pale skin. Shay's arm ached from how tightly he'd tied her arm. She tried to wiggle her fingers, but all she could feel was pins and needles from lack of blood in her arm... and his mouth. It was hot and soft and made that burning in her pelvis ignite. She hated it. All of it. Everything. The betrayal of her body, even though it was the drugs.

Alastor stretched to set the needle on the nightstand, his forearm finally releasing her chest so she could take a full breath. Shay was still pinned underneath him as he straddled her and held up the vial of blood.

"I told myself I wouldn't do this again." He glanced at her, licked his lips before throwing back the vial and drinking her blood. "Ah," Alastor groaned as he pressed the heel of his hand against his forehead. He threw the vial and it broke against the wall.

Shay had to admit, there was something sexy watching the Demon fall apart because of her. Alastor was always in control. Always. But it seemed once he swallowed her blood, he lost it. His eyes glazed over, his hips rocked like someone was riding him, his hands stretched into his hair, and there were drops of blood on his lips. This went on for a few minutes and Shay could only watch wide-eyed, feeling like she was at a male strip club and getting the lap dance of the century. Her blood burned, her body ached. She wanted him to touch her but hated him, never wanted to be in his presence ever again.

But then, Alastor's body went limp. His shoulders slumped and he fell to the side.

He'd fallen asleep in a drugged haze.

Shay exhaled a breath, more thankful than she'd ever been in her entire life as Alastor's still body lay next to hers, his mouth against her shoulder. She lay motionless until the drugs wore off and she could move her body. Little by little she shifted so as not to wake Alastor. She loosened the tie from her arm and flexed her fingers until the blood began flowing.

Shay scooted, inch by inch toward the edge of the mattress. Alastor shifted. Shay went still.

"Where do you think you're going?" he grabbed her wrist and pulled it toward his mouth. His eyes fluttered closed.

Shay was still as stone, waiting. His mouth on her wrist was all she could feel. His lips felt nothing like Jed's.

Warm tears dripped down Shay's face and into her hair. For the first time since Alastor had told her that Jed was dead, she cried. As silently as she could muster, the tears flowed and soaked her hair and the blanket under her head. All these days she'd tried not to think about how she'd lost everyone. Daddy, Momma, her home, and now Jed. Sure their relationship hadn't been easy, especially lately, but they had each other and he'd promised to do better. At least he was trying and so was she.

A stomach full of drugged blood kept Alastor asleep for the night. The Demon didn't notice the second time when Shay slipped her hand from his and edged herself away from him until her feet touch the floor. She stood at the foot of the bed, her gaze spanning the room, looking for something that could be of use. There was nothing. Whatever weapons Alastor had in the hovel, they weren't here.

Shay made her way toward the door, wiped her eyes, and left the room holding the tattered edges of her dress together.

THIRTY-SIX

Nero couldn't find Jed or Chel. Last he'd seen them they were on the road and Nero had been called to make a deal on the Earthen plane. He'd searched the area where he'd left Jed but there was no one, only the infrequent Demon or dead soul wandering.

Nero needed help and there was only one place he could go. He galloped full speed ahead toward the castle. Head down and hooves beating the road, he ran past mountains and valleys and Demon towns. He passed Safe Houses filled with Deacons and freshly dead souls repenting. He passed hordes of zombies who'd missed their chance to repent and were stuck and rotting in Hell. He passed familiar roads and towns until he could finally see the castle in the burning caves.

Nero slowed at the driveway and the Hellions let

him pass. He went to the courtyard and whinnied loudly, hoping someone would come out as he called over and over again.

The sun was coming up and Nero was getting antsy. He went to the large wooden door and kicked at it, neighing louder and more frequently. He kicked so hard splinters of wood popped off the door and littered the courtyard.

It finally opened.

The Hellion named Klaus was there, white beard and horns and looking extra grumpy.

Nero waved his head and snapped his teeth.

Klaus said something in Hellspeak. Unfortunately Nero couldn't speak that language either. He stomped his hooves and wagged his head toward the driveway, bit at Klaus's shirt and tried to drag him.

"Nah, don't do that beast." Klaus pushed his nose away. "Let me get the boss."

Nero paced the courtyard as he waited for the Hellions to return.

When he heard voices behind him, Nero turned to see a group of people. The Hellion Commander Skeele was there standing protectively close to Meg.

"What's with the horse?" Meg asked.

"He's acting strange," Klaus replied, tugging on his shirt. "Tried to tug me down the road."

Skeele stepped closer to Nero and held out a hand. "What's the problem? Where are Jed and Chel?"

Nero whinnied, wagged his head toward the road again. He trotted in a circle and tried to get them to follow but the Hellions and their Queen wouldn't budge.

"He's trying to tell us something," Meg said. "Something must've happened."

"Nero wouldn't leave Shay," Skeele said as he rubbed his chin.

Nero nickered and bobbed his head toward the road but they weren't understanding a thing.

"I think he wants us to go with him," Meg finally said.

Yes! Yes! Nero reared up the tiniest bit and whinnied with joy before turning away and galloping down the driveway. He paused to turn. No one was following.

Nero's only conclusion was that this group was too stupid to understand. Idiots, just staring. Had they never seen an animal trying to tell them something? Had they never watched Lassie? Nero had in the early days when Shay was nursing him back to life and Daddy and Momma let her bring him into the farmhouse. If people could understand a dog why couldn't they understand him?

Nero galloped back toward everyone and stared.

Communication was getting him nowhere. They were idiots as far as he was concerned. This was pointless.

"He wants someone to go," Meg said, pointing down the road. She walked closer to Nero and touched his shoulder. "Show me."

Nero stared for a moment into her eyes then turned, leading her away.

"You can't go," Skeele said as he strode to Meg's side.

"Someone has to," Meg said. "I ordered that Shay not be harmed and look what's happened. She's been kidnapped and you only allowed a skeleton crew to go find her."

Skeele stepped in front of Meg to stop her. "You can't go in your condition." He motioned to her abdomen. "You are staying here. They can figure it out."

"Send more Hellions," Meg said.

"No. They stay here to protect you." Skeele crossed his arms, holding his ground.

Meg mimicked his stance. "We owe it to Shay. She stood in for me when I was imprisoned; she put her life on the line for me. For us."

"And how do you think Shay would feel if something happened to you after she risked her life to save you?" Skeele asked.

Nero looked at Meg. She was pregnant. No, this

wouldn't do. Nero wouldn't bring the pregnant Queen of Hell on a rescue mission.

Nero whinnied a goodbye and galloped away. He needed help but Queen Meg and her Hellion Commander were too much drama for him to deal with. He shook his head in disgust. He missed the simpleness of life on the ranch when the greatest dilemma was Momma asking the ranch hands what they wanted for dinner and they muttered on and on about fried chicken and grilled steak and macaroni and cheese until she gave up and just made whatever she felt like. She always gave Nero a plate in secret on the back porch while everyone else was gathered around the dinner table. Yes, he missed the simple days.

Nero heard the beating of wings as Hellions took to the sky following him. He didn't bother to look up and see who it was.

Nero and Shay had gotten through plenty in their lives, this was just one more hurdle. Nero didn't need the others. He'd figure this out himself, just like when he hunted down Clyburn and killed him.

THIRTY-SEVEN

MORNING BROUGHT shame from only one of the parties. It wasn't Alastor. He was looking thoughtful as he chewed his breakfast and drank his coffee.

Shay had cooked for him, not because she wanted to but because it was expected of her.

Shay was sore and tired and felt as though she'd participated in something dirty and disgraceful. It wasn't by choice, but she felt shameful.

Alastor was vibrant and filled with energy. She assumed it had something to do with the blood he'd ingested. The shadows that lingered on his face were set and calm, revealing a Demon that some might consider handsome. He was freshly showered and had combed back his dark hair. He'd dressed in a black suit and looked ready to head out to business meetings for the day.

"I have a better plan now." Alastor wagged his fork in Shay's direction. "Now that I've tasted the goods." He winked and the shadows on his face darkened.

The interaction looked very much like a business proposition and Shay was sure Alastor had more than enough experience to con someone into agreeing with him.

Shay set her fork down, feeling disgusted.

"I think I'd like to keep you for myself. There are other things we can sell." He was focused on the bruise in the crook of her arm. "Your blood will replenish but other things won't." His dark eyes roamed over her as she stood to clear her dishes. "One of them could hurt you once they got a taste and then you'd be no use to me dead."

Shay washed her dishes in the sink and thought about how she might be able to kill Alastor. There were plenty of knives for cooking. She scanned the drawers wondering where he'd pulled the drugs from last night.

SHAY DIDN'T EXPECT it when Alastor left for the entire day. She was alone. Shay occupied her time with sleeping and snooping. She searched every drawer in the hovel, every closet. She found a book with runes and strange writing in Alastor's room. In his bathroom she found baggies of white powder behind the mirror. She took one and hid it in her pocket.

"What are you doing in here?" Alastor's voice said from behind her.

Shay stilled. "Cleaning." She turned with a cloth in her hand and pretended to wipe down the countertop.

"You're not the maid." Alastor was watching her warily.

"I was bored."

Alastor's brow rose and his lips tipped up. "If you're bored, there's plenty we can do."

"Not that bored." She moved to escape the bathroom but his big body blocked her.

"This is a good a place as any." He pointed to the counter. "Sit."

"I'd rather leave. I'm tired." Shay stepped to the side. She heard the clang of metal and glass and looked toward his hand. He wanted blood.

"You can sleep after."

"No."

"Sit." His gaze was threatening. "Sit or I will make you sit."

Shay watched him warily. He no doubt had been

wheeling and dealing all day long. He probably made some promises that he now had to deliver on them.

"I don't like this," Shay warned as she backed up, her back hitting the ledge of the counter.

"Doesn't matter." Alastor washed his hands in the sink and dried them on a clean towel from the shelf. It was a very human thing to do, almost clinical. And while Shay appreciated it, she still didn't like it.

"Sit. Now." Alastor demanded, his deep voice rising a few octaves.

Shay slid up on the counter and waited.

He didn't use a tie this time, he had a long piece of elastic which he knotted above her elbow.

Shay noticed four glass vials as she tried to ignore the pinch of the elastic.

"Don't move." Alastor positioned his body between her legs and leaned forward, crowding her. He pulled Shay's arm straight before sticking her with the needle.

Alastor filled the vials, hesitated for a moment before unknotting the elastic. He didn't have a bandage. Shay felt his mouth on her arm, his hot tongue on the spot where he'd punctured her skin.

Shay thought of Meg and Skeele and their blood bond. She closed her eyes. Shay didn't want that, definitely not with Alastor. She leaned away and considered a future in which she pretended to enjoy this and him and what he'd make her do. Shay couldn't see it.

His heat left her and Shay opened her eyes. Alastor had walked into his bedroom and retrieved a package.

"Put this on." He collected the vials of blood and tucked them into a leather case. "We have another party tonight."

Shay slid off the counter, feeling wobbly. She gripped the edge of the counter and steadied herself before taking the package and heading to her bathroom.

The dress was black, again, with a swirling embroidered pattern that looked like vines. It was sleeveless with a high neck, a slit to her hip that showed his brand marked on her skin.

Shay waited in the living room of the hovel until Alastor appeared at the front door. Apparently he'd left her alone while she readied herself.

"Do I get shoes tonight?" Shay asked.

"No." Alastor motioned for her to move. He led her to a different black Jeep. She was sure the other one was totaled after she'd made him drive it off the road and down the ravine. "Get in the back." Alastor's lips were pressed in a line. "I'd much rather have you in the front where I can see you, but I don't trust you after last time."

He drove to the black mansion again. There was a line of Demons entering. Alastor parked and got Shay out. She hissed as the sharp rocks from the driveway tore at her bare feet.

"I'll carry you." It was a command not an offer. "Can't have you bleeding all over the floor."

Alastor lifted Shay like she weighed nothing. She didn't want to touch him but for fear of falling, stretched an arm across his shoulders and gripped his suite jacket. He stopped just before the path turned smooth and set her down.

Shay flinched as the sharp rocks cut into her feet.

"Changed my mind," Alastor whispered. "You'll see why. Stay next to me, don't wander."

Since Alastor was considerably much taller than Shay, she had to skip to keep up with his stride and that only deepened the cuts on her feet. When they reached the steps to the black mansion, Shay was leaving bloody footprints everywhere she went.

It didn't take long to see what Alastor's plan was. There was no shame when the Demons at the party bent to swipe at her bloody footprints and taste. Shay was reminded of that brutal night in the barn when the Hellion recruits had come for her. She scanned the party. There had to be a hundred Demons packed in to the mansion. There was no saving her here. She moved closer to Alastor and he smirked as he chatted with two male Demons, glancing at her from the corner of his eye.

Alastor paraded Shay into every room, and in every room she left bloodied footprints. It felt very deliberate to Shay and she didn't like the feeling she got as some of the Demons bent to the floor and licked her blood like dogs. There were growls and howls and moans of delight. All made her considerably uncomfortable.

Worse was when one of the Demons licked her heel and she shrieked in surprise. Alastor dragged her away from the one who'd done it and threatened the Demon in Hellspeak.

By the time they reached the dining room, the bleeding had stopped. Coagulated gobs of blood trickled to nothing. Alastor brought her into the empty dining room and like last time, there were pedestals in the center of the room.

"Up." Alastor motioned for Shay to take the pedestal in the middle.

"You said you weren't going to do this again." Shay reminded him.

He patted his jacket pocket and Shay heard the *tink* of glass. "We're not selling you, just your blood. And now that they got a taste, they'll bid higher."

Alastor went to the door at the far end of the room and came back with two young women, the same as last time. They smiled at her. They were far too relaxed and Shay wondered if they'd been drugged like Alastor had done to her before. But, they were upright and walking and seemed in control of their bodies.

"Don't judge," the girl in red said. "Some of us like the auction and the thrill afterwards."

The girl to Shay's left clicked her tongue. "Some of us enjoy it quite a lot. Have you let him have you yet?" She tipped her chin toward Alastor. "That's the one I'd want."

Shay stared at Alastor as he opened the door and let the guests take their seats.

"Never," Shay replied to the girls. "Not over my dead body."

"So you won't mind if I offer myself to him?" the one in red asked.

"I don't care what he does." Shay held her head high as Alastor headed back toward the pedestals where the girls stood on display.

The girls stopped talking once Alastor got within earshot. He was working the crowd, chatting up the customers. Shay didn't understand any of it since he chose Hellspeak again. The whole night had been garbled speech that made her ears ache. She understood the laughs and the jeers and when Alastor took a protective stance when some got out of hand. The rest of it was gibberish.

The auction was enthusiastic for the other two girls.

But when Alastor held up the vials of blood, the room went wild.

There was roaring, keening, screaming, growling coming from the throats of the Demons in the seats. Some stood and shouted, all throwing their offers for more and more money at Alastor.

Shay glanced to him, a wide smile spread on his face, his chest puffed and he stood tall, reveling in the mounds of money the Demons were willing to pay him for a vial of Shay's blood. It sickened her.

When the auction was over, Alastor escorted Shay to the back room with the other girls.

He slapped her on the ass as she walked through the threshold. "Got a prime price for these." He held the vials, ready to distribute to their rightful owners.

The girls were watching her as Alastor closed the door.

"Is there a way out?" Shay asked, searching the room.

"It's a closet," the one in red said. "There's no way out."

"We searched it already. Alastor wouldn't risk putting us in an unsecure room," the other girl said, toying with her blonde hair.

Shay stared at them both, unbelieving. They didn't seem afraid or angry at all.

"You aren't here against your will?" Shay asked.

The blonde shook her head. "Don't judge me. Just because I don't desire the boys of the Earthen plane."

Shay blinked hard. Before she met Jed, she didn't know there was anything else besides the Earthen plane, and she'd never called it that. Just planet earth or home. To know that there were people who knew about Hell and Demons blew her mind. She never thought she'd lived a sheltered life, but the more she saw, the more she decided she must have.

"Not everyone is a princess," the one in the red dress said. "Before the Zombie War, I was a mess. Stripping for five-dollar bills just to put food on the table." She stretched and spun in a circle, showing off her dress. "Now I get pampered every week."

The door opened. Alastor called, "Red, let's go."

"Toodles," she said as she waved at Shay and the blonde before leaving.

The blonde was fixing her hair. "Take Alastor for a ride. You know what they say..."

"I certainly don't," Shay replied.

"Once you go Demon, you never go back." She was standing by the door as it opened and winked at Shay as she left.

Shay paced the room. She was definitely not going to *go Demon*. The thought made her gag, no matter how nice Alastor ever treated her, he'd kidnapped her and killed her boyfriend. If she went anything with a Demon, it would be to kill him.

Alastor left Shay in the room alone long enough for her to get nervous about what was going on and if he'd ever come back. She paced the small room. Sat, stood, paced some more. She leaned against the walls and listened for voices. She ran her hands over the plaster panels and pressed, searching for hidden doors. There was nothing.

When the door finally opened, Alastor was leaning against the frame like he could barely stand.

"What the fuck?" Shay snapped at him. "I've been in here forever."

Alastor's eyes were half-lidded as he motioned for her to follow. His movements were slow, relaxed, very unlike his usual demeanor.

The mansion was empty. Small creatures were cleaning and rearranging as Alastor led her to the front door. They left; the Jeep they'd arrived in was the only vehicle remaining.

Shay stopped at the sharp rocks and glanced to where the Jeep was parked. She considered walking at a snail's pace to prevent the rocks from cutting up her feet.

Alastor noticed. He lifted her without warning and held her close. "You made some good money tonight." He smelled like whiskey and smoke.

Shay turned away as the heat of his breath brushed her cheek.

"You were such a good girl. I should get you a present." He stopped at the Jeep and opened the door.

"I don't need a present. I need to be let the fuck out of this situation." She squeaked as he tossed her onto the seat.

Alastor slammed the door closed and walked to the driver side. "You pay the debts you owe," he said as he got in and started the vehicle.

"Should you be driving?" Shay asked from the backseat. "You smell like a dive bar."

"I'm fine." The Jeep jerked as he hit the brake at an awkward moment then hit the curb.

"You're going to kill us." Shay buckled her seatbelt.

Alastor shrugged. "No different than you."

Shay spent the ride through the mountains gripping the doorhandle and pressing herself against the seat, bracing for impact.

When Alastor parked at the hovel, he let her out and said, "See, not a blemish on your hide." His dark gaze drifted over her.

Shay ran inside to the bathroom and locked the door. She washed the dried blood off her feet and showered the sweat off her back and tried to figure a way out of this mess she was in.

Thirty-Eight

Nero was pissed. Steam rose from his nostrils as he galloped. There was only one more place he could go for help. The chapel in the graveyard.

Nero whinnied as he galloped, like a firetruck with sirens blaring. He paced at the fence, stomping the grass and dirt until the door opened. The morning sun was coming over the treetops but the graveyard still had a coating of fog over the grass.

Noah was wearing pajama pants with no shirt and carrying a cup of coffee. "What's all the racket about?" he hollered to Nero. "You got a Demon foot up your ass or are you just happy to see me?" Noah flinched as his bare feet hit the wet grass. He walked closer and opened the gate.

Nero moved to enter the fenced yard but he was too big to fit through the gate opening.

"Back up big boy." Noah held up a hand motioning for him to reverse. "What brings you by at the crack of early-as-fuck-dawn? You're going to wake Thrush sounding off like that."

Nero went still. He felt stupid for coming here. The baby... Noah couldn't come with him, he had a family to protect.

"Cat got your tongue?" Noah asked, sipping at his coffee with raised brows.

"Ah, Nero," Nightingale's light voice called out from the stoop.

Nero felt more stupid. What was he doing here? Why did he think these people could help him? Noah and Nightingale were technically ghosts but something drew him here.

Noah's eyes narrowed on the Demon horse. "You're supposed to be on a mission to rescue Shay. What're you doing here?"

Nero whinnied as though the noise told the entire story, everything he couldn't say with words.

Noah pressed his lips together and tipped his head with a few nods, like he understood every stuttered sound that left Nero's throat. But then he said, "Got no clue, buddy. Not a frickin' clue."

Nightingale slipped in front of Noah and held her hand out.

Nero hesitated. He knew the dead Angel woman had been brought back from elsewhere. He'd heard enough conversations about Nightingale visiting people in their dreams, he'd heard about her defeating the Nightjar to save her little boy, Thrush. Nightingale had an energy and power that caused Nero to take a step back. He could sense she was something *different*.

"I won't hurt you, Nero." Nightingale whistled a light trill. She sounded like a bird. "Touch me and I'll see what I can understand from you."

Nero hesitated, but he didn't have much of a choice, time was running out. He set his snout in her palm.

Noah's lips pressed together and his expression elicited a sense that this was bullshit.

Nero looked away from Noah and focused on Nightingale. Her eyes were closed, her face flexed in concentration.

Nightingale's hand fell away and Nero felt hopeless for a moment, anticipating nothing.

"He's lost them," Nightingale said. "He can't find Jed or Chel but he knows where Shay is. He just needs help. This Demon he's up against is strong." She pet Nero's cheek. "He doesn't want to hurt Shay again."

Noah made a face of agreement.

"Give me a minute." Nightingale's hand left Nero and she closed her eyes. "Some get really mad when I do this so you'll have to apologize for me."

Nero looked to Noah for an explanation but the man was staring into his coffee cup. "Meg wants me to fetch her pancakes," he muttered. "Christ, I just want one morning to drink my coffee in peace."

Nightingale's eyes flashed open. "Jed and Chel are in Hell. I'm not sure where, but their minds are... *slowed*." Nightingale took a deep breath. "You need to find them before it's too late, Nero."

Nero nodded his head silently, his mane flying in the morning sun.

"Thrush is awake." Nightingale was watching Nero warily. "We can't go with you but I know you will find them. You can do this Nero. You're a Crossroads Demon, you haven't even realized half of your power."

Nero nickered lightly as he turned to gallop away. He'd learned one thing from all of his recent interactions, these people weren't much help at all and Shay deserved better.

You haven't even realized half of your power. Nero wondered what Nightingale had meant.

Thirty-Nine

THERE WAS MUSIC PLAYING. Shay recognized it as Michael Jackson's Smooth Criminal. Alastor was drunk. Wasted. He was stumbling through the kitchen searching the cabinets, bobbing along to the beat of the music.

"Ah. Shay-baby. There you are." He danced over to her, moonwalk and all. It was ridiculous how well he danced.

"Don't call me that." The only people allowed to call her Shay-baby were Daddy and Jed and they were both dead. Thanks to Demons.

"Don't be so cruel." He was swaying, moving to the beat of the song. If Shay didn't dislike him so much she might find it endearing. "Come on." He grabbed her hips and pulled her closer.

"Don't touch me." Shay slapped at his chest. His fingers brushed the brand on her hip and Shay hissed in shock.

"Look at us. We could take over the world together. You've done so well as my pet. You could be more. Like the others. You might like it."

He kept touching her; hands on her waist, pulling her closer, rubbing himself against her.

Shay slapped him across the face. Hard.

"You fucking bitch!" Alastor shouted. His eyes were black as pitch and filled with rage.

Shay stood her ground. "I told you to stop."

"After all this time, all these weeks. I've given you everything." His hands were pinching her hips as she struggled to back away from him. "So much more than all the others. I've never allowed them the freedoms you have. I treated you better."

"No!" Shay shouted back. "You've taken everything from me. You ruined my life. I hate you. I hate everything that you are and what you've done to me." Shay was filled with rage. "You and your kind have killed everyone that I love." Shay was shaking and she could barely think straight.

"You want me to treat you like shit, treat you like cattle? Like a dog? I can do that." He backhanded her.

Shay wasn't ready for it, and her vision turned red as

she flew across the room and hit the wall. She could barely move.

Alastor was on her before she could stand. He grabbed a handful of blue hair and dragged her up. "Your blood is enough." He dragged her to his bedroom and threw her on the bed. "If this is what you want, this is what you get."

Blood dripped into Shay's left eye. Her mind felt fuzzy and she figured she'd cut herself when she hit the wall. She rolled, tried to crawl off the bed but Alastor came back with rope. He tied her wrists and ankles, pulling the rope tight to the bedframe.

"You're a bastard," Shay said, fighting him and losing. He was too big and too strong.

"I embrace it."

Shay tried to kick at him with her knees but Alastor held her leg down, his grip painful on her right leg. His thumb touched the scar there.

"I have a feeling you've a demon inside you also, little human. That's the only conclusion I can come to with this scar and that Crossroads Demon connection." Alastor was staring for minutes before he released her and moved to the table near the bed. Glass and metal clinked together.

He took her blood, vials and vials until she felt dizzy and weak and she couldn't fight him when his mouth touched her arm and licked and licked and licked until it clotted. When he was done, she could see the bulge in his groin through half-lidded eyes and feared what would come next.

If she had her pistol she'd shoot him. If she had a lasso of rope she'd choke him. She couldn't do any of that in her current state.

Alastor didn't touch her again. Thank God. He was a bastard but at least he had some type of morals that stopped him from touching her below the belt.

He was lounging across the room where he'd stumbled onto a dressing bench. Shay swallowed hard as she watched him, inebriated and high on blood. He slid off the bench near the closet and rolled onto his back, hands in his hair as he watched the ceiling. He was imagining someone was there, touching him, groping him, riding him. It was indecent. Shay turned away and focused on the rope that tied her wrists. She tried tugging but the knot only got tighter. She scooted up, hoping to get to the knot with her teeth, but the ropes at her ankles tightened.

Shay stretched her fingers, trying to reach the ends of the rope or loosen the knot. She tried until her arms and back ached and she fell asleep.

In the morning, Alastor left the bathroom with a towel wrapped low around his waist and made his way to the closet. He'd taken a handful of phone calls since he scraped himself off the floor. He'd taken more of Shay's blood as soon as he woke up and threatened to be back soon.

Shay eavesdropped on his phone calls. He was selling her blood and getting more money than he would have for her body.

It went on for days. More vials of blood than Shay could count. She wished for a Crossroads Demon call just so she could escape the bedroom and the needle Alastor kept sticking in her veins.

Shay soon found herself sleeping more than she was awake. The pinch of the needle barely triggered her to open her eyes. Her mouth was dry, and she'd never been so thirsty. Her eyes felt like sand had been rubbed in them. Shay's arms and legs felt like lead; moving was too much effort. Alastor hadn't given her more than a bite of bread and a sip of water since he'd started draining her. She was weak, wasting away.

"You want what?" Alastor's deep voice pulled Shay from slumber. "No. That's not part of the deal...." Alastor was staring at her as he talked into the phone. "I won't offer that." He was making a face, his brow creased. "How much?" There was a long silence as he pinched the bridge of his nose before looking at her again. "Fine. It's a deal but if you do anything more than take her blood, I'll kill you myself."

Shay closed her eyes, not caring what the deal was. She felt the bed shift as Alastor sat next to her. He touched her hair, then her torn shirt.

"It wasn't supposed to be like this."

"Fuck off," Shay croaked.

Alastor gripped her chin and forced Shay to look at him. "I wanted more from you."

Shay glared, unfeeling, too tired to say anything.

"I had better plans. The other girls..." he was searching her dull eyes, "aren't as valuable as you." He licked his lips. "Don't taste as sweet..."

Shay thought Alastor was trying to confess something but his words tumbled then jumbled then turned into Hellspeak and she could no longer understand him. It didn't matter, the more time she spent in Hell the harder it was to figure out the rules that governed this place. Just like the human world, there was sin and evilness, little accountability, few laws that mattered. Shay decided all the realms were pretty much a cluster fuck. The scar on her thigh ached right down to the bone. Shay worried that the lack of blood might weaken her leg. She didn't have anyone to heal her out here in the wilderness of Hell. If something happened–heck, if this got any worse–she was good as dead.

FORTY

Nero galloped through Hellscape. He ran paths down to dirt between the trees, trampled grass, searched every scrap of land he came across. He couldn't find Jed or the Hellion.

They were here. He could feel it in his center. They were here in the echoes of the leaves when the wind blew and the movement of shadows from the corner of his eye. Some strange magic had them trapped. Their shadows disappeared like morning mist. He could smell them. He saw their nearly dirt-filled footprints and traces of their travels; scuff marks in the soil, broken branches, and then all trace of them stopped and there was nothing. Hellforest and its paths became quiet as fresh fallen snow and just as secretive. The only thing Nero found was a large rock that looked out of place. The Demons and Nero had curled a path around it in both directions.

Nero huffed in frustration as another sunset appeared. He'd been searching for Jed and the Hellion for days and weeks. He'd been back from making the deal on the Earthen plane with one desire; to save Shay. But he couldn't do it alone. He needed help. He needed Jed's magic and the Hellion's strength. He wouldn't risk hurting her again. The incident at the barn was enough to haunt him forever. When those young Hellions came for Shay, hunting her, Nero had injured her while fighting with them. No, Nero wouldn't go for that again. He needed help to ensure that Shay was safe and saved.

Nero stopped at a meandering path that led to a pub. They had been here, long ago. There were traces of the men. Nero stood in the path and watched the Demons come and go from the front door. He wondered if Jed and the Hellion were in there. Nero's head tracked back and forth slowly as he made the decision. The golden chain strung from his ear to his throat jingled as his head moved. He walked closer, judging the size of the door, sure that he could make it through.

The door opened as a Demon walked through and didn't close all the way. He moved forward, leaving hoofprints in the path. He nudged the door with his snout until it opened, then walked through.

Nero had to dip his head under the threshold of the door and squeeze his flank to get inside, but it was worth the look on all the Demons' faces. Nero knew horses didn't walk into pubs. They didn't walk into many places like he just had but he didn't care. Nero wasn't a normal horse and too much was on the line for animal politeness.

All heads turned.

Clop. Clop. Clop. Nero's footsteps echoed on the hard floor as he neared the bar. He wasn't sure who to approach, but the Demon on the other side of the bar looked authoritative. Nero walked right up, shoved the barstools aside with this big body, tilted his head, and stared at the Demon bartender with one large black eye.

"What do you want horse?" the bartender asked.

Nero huffed.

The bartender stared.

The pub was silent.

Nero nickered. He couldn't speak otherwise so he tried a variety of noises that he could make with this throat.

"Are ya looking for food?" the bartender asked.

Nero huffed.

The bartender filled a mug with beer and set it in front of Nero, then set a brick of cheese next to the mug.

Nero sniffed. He'd tried beer. The ranch hands would give it to him on the Fourth of July and Christmas, late at night when Nicholas and the rest of the family were asleep. Meanwhile, the ranch hands were awake with loneliness wandering the ranch all thoughtful and depressed. Nero knew what beer tasted and smelled like, and what the bartender had set in front of him was not right. There was a murky scent. Nero's eyes blew wide as he realized what had happened.

It was poisoned!

Nero hit the mug with his snout. Beer spilled and the murky scent spread. Nero whinnied a noise that was filled with *rage*.

He slammed his front hooves on the bar top, splintering the wood. He shivered, felt the quiver of electricity under his skin. He shivered harder, gnashed his teeth together, tensed his body, and *changed*. Nero was already huge but in that second he doubled in size, his long black tail and mane becoming stiff as needles and sharp as razorblades. His veins became giant ropes of obsidian, twining and swirling under his skin like protective armor. The hunger was the worst part.

Nero was a thrashing beast in a small box. He broke everything wooden, everything with bones. His hooves were sharp, stabbing and cutting, his legs a power to be reckoned with. He blocked the door so none of the Demons could escape. When they charged, he killed them. When they jabbed their weapons at him, he killed them. When they looked at him, he killed them.

And when he was done destroying, he ate them. The sound of their bones crunching between his teeth echoed through Hellscape like a lightning storm. The only thing that remained of the pub was bloodstains and splintered timber. He came across a smoky glass jar that smelled like the poison from the beer and cheese. Something clicked in Nero's throat, a strange power he'd never called upon. He whinnied something wrath-filled and fire came out, burning the jar of potion, flames licking the blood soaked floorboards.

He huffed and cleared his throat, shook until the shiver returned his body to something less frightening.

He roamed from what was left of the pub as it turned to ash, stopping at the end of the path and turning his ears, searching for the sound of Jed's voice. He heard the deep timbre in the distance and galloped toward it.

FORTY-ONE

LAYERS OF ROCK dust had solidified on the men. They resembled a strange formation of granite dropped by a glacier as it passed the Hellscape eons ago. Pitted and stained green with forest mildew, the men had been trapped for far too long but not as long as one might think. The potion had accelerated their solidification. They didn't know but their thoughts had become as slow as their movements and they'd turned to stone unknowingly.

But then, everything suddenly shifted. Rock crumbled and fell away from the men. Jed felt the fog lift from his mind and the weight lift from his shoulders.

Chel's wings no longer dragged as though weighed down by bricks. He flexed the bat-like appendages and groaned. "I feel like I've been sleeping under a mountain."

"Something's changed," Jed said, turning to Chel and stretching his hands in front of him.

"The mother potion has been wasted. Something's coming," Chel said, turning to glance behind them as the ground shook.

Jed kicked a lump of stone. No. The realization came to him that they never made it to the pub. They hadn't made it more than a few hundred feet before becoming encased in stone. He wasn't sure how much time had passed. How much time they'd missed. How long had Shay been left with Alastor...

Nero's happy whinny echoed.

"Finally." Jed rubbed his face as the fog cleared.

Nero was running toward them.

"Where have you been?" Chel asked the horse. "We've been waiting for you to come back for ages."

Nero was bobbing his head and huffed. He jerked his head in the direction of the hovel in the mountains and nudged Jed to get moving.

"We're not going back to the pub to confront them?" Chel asked.

Nero hollered, showing his teeth and stomping. He rubbed his flank against Jed, urging him to climb up.

Jed jumped, muscles weak from disuse, and he

almost didn't make it onto Nero's back. His legs ached as he stretched and pulled himself straight.

Chel leapt to launch himself into the air but he stumbled and fell down on one knee. "How long were we trapped in rock?" Chel asked. "My wings can barely hold me."

"Too long." Jed wrapped his hands in Nero's mane, fingers feeling numb from weeks without motion. "You want me to carry you?" Jed asked with a smirk.

"I'd rather crawl." Chel stood and launched himself into the air. He flew, lopsided for a few beats until he had enough force to right himself.

Jed laughed from the path where Nero galloped.

FORTY-TWO

"They're coming for you," the dark haired woman said in Shay's dream.

"Who?" Shay no longer believed anyone was going to help her. She was in a bad place. A terrible place that no human would ever come back from.

Cold hands touched her face. "Hang on for just a little bit longer." Dark eyes searched hers. "Please, Shay."

———

Shay was being lifted. Her arms ached but they were no longer tied down. She was wearing something new, a dress, the black one. Alastor had changed her clothing.

"You've sold me," she mumbled. "I'm going to die here."

"No," Alastor's voice was stern, "this is part of your repayment. Krelp has clear instructions to only feed, nothing more. He's very wealthy and is paying a prime price for you."

"You suck," was all Shay could muster to say to him.

A sly smile crossed Alastor's face. "Perhaps I do, but the other girls don't think I'm so bad."

"They're stupid." Shay wanted to walk but she couldn't find the energy to struggle and get out of his arms. "You've done something to them."

"I gave them money and freedom," Alastor said.

"Your skin trades are not freedom. I remember the chains and the tents where you kept me the first time."

Alastor didn't reply.

They were at another mansion, black brick with three stories. Alastor carried Shay inside and a butler of sorts escorted them down hallways and stairs before pointing to a closed door. "He's expecting you."

Alastor stepped forward, easing Shay through the doorway.

Shay heard the scuttling sound of claws on hardwood, the *shhhhh*-sweep of wings dragging.

"Finally," a gravelly voice said. "Put her there."

A wet sound filled the air as Krelp licked his chops, eager.

Shay saw the lair in slow blinks, too tired to keep her heavy eyes open. She wondered if Alastor had drugged her again or if she was weak from being drained of blood daily.

"Put her there. Put her there!" Krelp clambered. Wings and limbs lobbed across the floor.

Alastor paused. "We have a deal," he reminded Krelp as he hesitated to lay Shay on the table.

"Yes, yes. Yes. Just a taste. Just a feast on the skin." Hands were rubbing together.

"No feasting on the skin!" Alastor shouted.

"Yes. No skin. No skin." Krelp was close to the table, he rapped on the wood with his fist. "Put her here. Give me what I paid for."

"Money first." Alastor held Shay, refusing to put her down.

Krelp began muttering in Hellspeak then reached in his pocket and pulled out a sack of coins. He slammed it on the table. "I'm hungry. Give her to me."

Shay's eyes fluttered open as Alastor set her down on the table and helped Krelp with the bindings to hold her in place. Then he left.

In the dimly lit chamber of the Demon's lair, Shay found herself bound and helpless, her heart pounding with fear as she awaited her grim fate. This was the end. She could feel it. Alastor had threatened the Demon but it was a malevolent creature hungry for blood. That was easy to see.

The air hung heavy with the stench of decay as the Demon approached, its form cloaked in shadows that seemed to writhe and twist with a sinister energy. Krelp's eyes glowed with an unholy light, fixated on Shay with an insatiable hunger that sent shivers down her spine. The creature was malformed with extra limbs that draped on the ground, boneless and limp.

Shay's breath caught in her throat as the Demon drew closer, its taloned fingers reaching out to brush against her skin with a chilling touch. She recoiled, the cold tendrils of fear wrapping around her heart like icy chains.

"You are mine now," the Demon hissed, its voice a guttural rasp that sent a panicked shiver downs Shay's spine. "Your blood will sustain me, human."

Shay's heart raced with panic as she struggled against her bindings, her mind racing with desperate thoughts. The chains that bound her were unyielding, their iron grip a cruel reminder of her captivity and all that she'd lost.

She prayed to be called away by the Crossroads but at the same time she feared Alastor's reaction if she fucked this up for him. She regretted making him angry. Look at where that had gotten her. Shay's skin crawled as she watched Krelp drooling over her.

Krelp ran his fingers along her skin, muttering in Hellspeak, his tongue lolling between his lips. He began licking her wrist slowly, then moved up her arm, tasting, probing for thick veins to feed from.

"He's used these ones already." Krelp's tongue pressed on the veins in her inner elbow. He licked up to her shoulder. She saw the gleam of a knife as he slid it under her dress and cut the fabric. "Mmmm. You taste like the Earthen plane. Like forbidden fruit." His tongue lathed over her collarbone.

Shay's body began trembling uncontrollably.

"Are you cold, my sweet?"

Shay slammed her eyes closed, thankful that he'd stopped licking her for a moment. "Yes," she replied, hoping to distract him.

"Let me light the fire. Don't want your blood turning to ice. I like it warm like soup."

Krelp slumped away, crossing the lair and starting a fire in the fireplace. The heat helped but didn't make the situation any better.

"There, my sweet." He'd returned to her side too quickly. His taloned fingers toyed with the pieces of her dress that he'd cut. He began licking her again, starting at her shoulder. Soon fingers were in her hair and he jerked her head to the side, revealing the smooth skin of Shay's neck.

"Yes. Yes. The sweet blood comes from here." A hand pressed against the vee of her thighs. "And here. Which would you have me feed from, my sweet?"

"Up here," Shay whispered, disgusted with the thought of him near another part of her body.

As the Demon prepared to sink its fangs into shay's flesh, a surge of defiance welled within her. With a trembling voice she summoned every ounce of courage she possessed, refusing to surrender to the darkness that threatened to consume her.

"You will not touch me," Shay declared, her voice trembling yet defiant. "I am not your prey."

The Demon only laughed, a cruel and mocking sound that echoed through the chamber like a death knell. With a swift motion, it seized Shay's wrist, its talons piercing her skin as it prepared to feed.

In that moment of desperation, Shay closed her eyes and tried to summon a glimmer of hope amidst the despair that threatened to engulf her. She refused to give in, clung to the belief that somehow, someway, she would find a way to escape this.

Krelp bit her, hard, and there was nothing nice about it.

Shay cried out as his fangs stabbed into her neck. She struggled against the bindings.

Krelp's taloned hand moved to her neck and held her steady.

Shay's body felt colder than ever; the heat of the fire did nothing to melt the ice in her veins. Krelp's grip tightened on the base of her neck as he fed.

He finally pulled away, blood smearing his lips. His eyes were big and black, and he seemed to grow before her.

"More," Krelp said, his taloned fingers roving her body, searching. The knife appeared again and he began cutting her dress. Slice by slice he exposed more of her body. Licking his lips, he bit her in other places; her wrist, her ankle, her stomach, her hip. He paused at the scar on her thigh.

"This is for me. This is mine." His knife pressed against the scar.

"No! No!" Shay screamed. "Don't touch me." She screamed as loud as she could, hoping someone would hear her. She was so afraid that Krelp would cut open the scar and release the Demon poison, afraid it would forever change her. And... deep down, she was afraid she'd lose her connection to Nero if it was gone.

Shay screamed louder.

FORTY-THREE

Pain rippled down the tether that connected Shay and Nero. Shay was terrified and in pain. Something bad was happening.

Nero's eyes blew wide, his whinny sounding like a roar as he put his head down and ran faster.

Chel couldn't keep pace from the sky. His batlike wings whipped harder and harder through Hellsky but he was getting further and further behind. All he could do was follow the shaking of the trees as Nero blasted past them.

"Whoa. Whoa!" Jed shouted, doing his best to hang on to Nero as he sped lighting fast through the forest then the winding mountain roads. The horse was moving so fast he was feeling queasy. "Don't drop me," Jed said.

Nero didn't slow, he only moved faster. His hooves pounded into the ground, dirt and leaves flying into the air leaving a cloud of debris in his wake.

Nero felt Shay scream again. The tether drew him in a different direction. Not towards the Demon's hovel in the mountains.

He galloped through winding mountain roads, up and up until a dirt road led to a clearing and a black brick mansion loomed before them.

Nero slammed his front hooves on the door to the mansion and it blew open. Wood and brick shattered. Nero neighed and it sounded like a roar.

Shay's screams echoed through the mansion. Nero followed the sound. Somewhere along the way, Jed had fallen off his back.

Chel landed outside the black mansion. He was running, pausing only to help Jed to his feet and follow Nero. Chel's Hellion blade was drawn as he entered.

Jed was close behind, his fingertips spurting lightning. He heard Shay's screams.

"Shay!" Jed shouted.

Then the deluge began. Lesser Demons began coming through the doors of the mansion.

Nero was near the stairwell, fighting off a handful of small, birdlike creatures.

Chel and Jed fought clusters of Demons.

Chel's blade cut through them like butter. Jed's magic slayed the ones that missed the blade and the ones Nero's hooves hadn't stomped to death. They met at the stairwell and began running down. They could hear Shay's screams and other strange noises.

"Shay!" Jed shouted again.

They followed the sound of her shrieks; she was close, but there were so many doors in this dungeon. Nero and Chel and Jed began kicking open every door they came across.

On the last one, Nero slammed his hooves on a door and it crumpled under his weight.

Jed stormed into the room, his aura blazing blue, arcane energy streaming from his fingertips.

Shay was there.

Jed recognized Alastor immediately. He was fighting with a deformed Demon that had blood on his mouth.

Alastor was standing next to Shay, protectively. She was tied down, bleeding, pale, her clothing ripped to shreds.

"Kill them!" Shay shouted.

She didn't have to ask twice.

Jed went for Alastor.

Chel went for Krelp.

Nero went for Shay, and he bit at the ropes holding her until they broke and she could sit up. Shay cried, wrapped her arms around Nero's neck and held on as he dragged her to her feet. Nero nickered lightly and licked her hands.

Krelp was stronger now that he had fresh blood in his gut. He moved quick, sidestepping and spinning away from Chel's blade. His taloned fingers swept out to scratch at Chel's body. Chel took his time, unfamiliar with this Demon and what powers he could have.

The room was crammed with furniture and trinkets, which Krelp took advantage of, using lamps and chairs as weapons against Chel. His dragging extra appendages found life and the Demon suddenly had five arms.

Chel guarded his head, ducked behind a couch to figure out a plan as the barrage of items flew past him and into the couch.

Energy crackled from Jed's fingertips. As he whispered a spell that sounded like ink and bone on parchment, tendrils of energy came from his hands and wrapped around Alastor.

They'd fought before, and Alastor didn't forget. He aimed well, aimed for Jed's hands and mouth as he ran toward Jed, punching. Alastor pulled the knife from under his jacket and cut Jed on the wrist.

Magic sputtered with the injury to his left arm.

Alastor shook his knife at Jed. "You won't defeat me again."

Jed smirked as the wound on his wrist healed with a quick charm. Sparks and energy intensified, wrapping around Alastor's body.

Alastor had his own weapons and he was more powerful than anyone in the room realized. But that's what happens when your father was Lucifer and your birthright was chaos and darkness, primed for eons. Alastor chanted in Hellspeak and the ground under their feet opened up. Just like at the campground on the Earthen plane, lesser Demons and strange creatures began crawling out. Cockroaches and spiders and black beetles swarmed Jed and Chel, biting and scratching, bringing chaos and destruction.

Nero slammed his front hooves on the table where Shay had been bound, splintering the wood. Shay dropped to the ground under Nero, covering her face. Slivers and splinters took to the air, stabbing through the lesser Demons. Nero shivered, felt the quiver of electricity under his skin. He shivered harder, gnashed his teeth together, tensed his body, and *changed*. Nero doubled in size, his long black tail and mane became stiff and sharp as razorblades. His veins, ropes of obsidian, twined and swirled under his skin like protective armor.

Shay changed forms too and Jed saw her like that for the first time. His eyes blew wide as he took her in. She was tall, hair so blue, eyes darker than night. She wasn't a terrifying Demon like her horse, no, she was a warrior; intimidating and absolutely stunning.

Lesser Demons grappled at Jed's legs like cockroaches. He cast a spell to disperse them.

Alastor got the upper hand, swinging a chair at his head. Jed kneeled to the ground, stunned.

Shay was closest to Krelp and killed him like she'd trained her whole life to do so. Her hand wrapped around his voluminous neck, squeezing until his spine broke. She threw the body on the floor. Silent communication went to Nero.

Nero opened his mouth, roared, and flames came out, setting Krelp's body on fire.

Jed's mouth went dry as he watched. It was a disruption he didn't need. He'd have to do better when Shay was around and they were entombed in battle. Alastor launched himself at Jed, wrapping around his legs and dragging Jed down until he dropped. Jed's head hit the ground, arcane energy swirling around his body as he used a wind-like force to throw Alastor away. Jed rose to his feet, blood dripping down the side of his head. Alastor was running toward him again.

"Clotpole!" Chel shouted.

It was a distraction and a secret communication. Chel tossed the basilisk tooth knife to Jed then launched himself at Alastor's legs, dragging him to the ground.

Jed caught the blade, gripped it tightly in his palm, ran, and leapt to Alastor's falling body. He dropped to a knee and jabbed the blade into Alastor's heart, just as the Demon had done to him weeks ago.

Alastor went still. The creatures stopped coming from the hole in the ground.

"Burn it all," Shay said with an angry growl.

Nero opened his mouth to comply, whinnied something that sounded like curse words and an oath upon the mansion and creatures that lived within the structure. Fire lit the room.

FORTY-FOUR

A SHIVER of electricity ran down Shay's spine at the exact moment it ran down Nero's. They both transformed back to normal.

"Kill him with fire," Shay said.

Flames lit Alastor's clothing as the basilisk tooth blade in his heart kept him immobile.

"We must leave or we'll die here also," Chel was urging the group toward the door. They ran down the hall and up the winding stairs, finding their way out of the black mansion.

They ran down the grand entry stairs, no longer being followed by lesser Demons or spiders or cockroaches.

They stopped to catch their breath.

"You came for me," Shay couldn't hide the glimmer in her eyes.

Nero whinnied a response that sounded like, "what did you expect us to do, leave you?"

Chel laughed, wrapped his arms around Shay and lifted her, spinning her. "We would have made it sooner if your boyfriend hadn't been picking fights in the pub."

Shay giggled as Chel set her on her feet. "That doesn't sound like the Jed I know."

She turned to kiss Jed and fall into his arms, but as she stepped toward him she noticed he looked awfully pale, too much blood was dripping from the side of his head and the cuts on his body.

Jed gave a little smirk. "Sorry about that–"

He dropped to the ground, a knife stuck under his shoulder blade.

"No! No, no, no, no..." Shay was scrambling to Jed's lifeless body, She dropped to her knees trying to roll him.. "No! I just got you back." She gripped the blade. "It's Alastor's. He always carried it on him."

"Leave it," Chel warned. "He'll bleed out if you remove it."

Nero was nudging Shay's shoulder. "Help me move him. I can't lift him."

"I'll fly him back," Chel said as he lifted Jed's limp body.

"No, Nero is faster." Shay patted Nero's back.

"With both of you?" Chel asked.

"Yes." Shay was certain. "He could carry a hundred people and be faster than you." She paused for a split second. "Don't take that personal."

Chel draped Jed's body over Nero's back.

Shay climbed up and held onto Jed and Nero's mane. She clicked her tongue. "Go fast!"

Nero took off with a thunderbolt.

FORTY-FIVE

Nero was faster than lightning, faster than the speed of light, faster than a black hole. Trees bent away from him before he passed them, hoofprints appeared in the soil before his gallop hit the ground. The ground in the distance shook before the black blur passed. Demons gaped, wondering what it was.

Chel took to the sky but all he saw was a blur, the shudder of the forest, the sound of thunder in the distance. Then nothing. He flew as fast as he could but he'd never keep up.

Shay held onto Jed. Blood soaked their clothing. Alastor's knife was embedded so deep in his back, it never moved with the force of Nero's gallop.

Shay leaned down, her upper body covering Jed's protectively as Nero ran. She whispered things to him, wished she could whisper a spell to keep him alive just as he'd done for her, but Shay didn't have magic like Jed. She had her words though.

"I have loved you since the moment I saw you at that Casino in Lame Deer and you dropped your French toast when you saw me. I have never felt this for anyone." Shay was gazing at his face. "I thought I'd never see you again after the Casino was under siege, but I did. You found me. You found me and charmed my parents and helped me when they died." Tears were streaming down her face. She wiped them away. "Please don't die. Please. Stay with me."

Shay's fingers stretched into his hair, tangled and tugging like she was trying to pull him back from death by the strands. Her leg wrapped around his, holding him tightly to Nero's side. She wouldn't let him fall. No matter how much he disappointed her, no matter how badly he'd hurt her with his fluttering back and forth. Shay wouldn't let him fall and she prayed that he'd notice and see the light and make the change within his own heart. Because Shay couldn't watch him die.

Blue hair fluttered like waves. The Hellions saw the blue blur before they saw the dark stallion. They smelled the blood before they saw Nero's passengers.

Skeele was waiting at the doors to the castle in the burning mountains, worried that something dark was coming for Meg. He was always overprotective. Always watching the doors and the perimeter.

Nero skidded to a stop.

Shay leapt off Nero's back, threadbare dress blowing in the wind. "Jed needs the infirmary. Can you get Teari?" There was panic in her voice, tears dried on her face, blood dried on her arms.

Skeele was no idiot. He realized the severity of the situation once he saw Shay was freed and Jed's bleeding body on Nero's back.

"Move him," Skeele ordered the nearby Hellions.

Klaus and Tukka were quick to gently move Jed and carry him into the castle.

Shay tried to follow them but Skeele held up a hand, stopping her.

"Where is Chel?" Skeele asked.

Shay pointed to the sky. "He's on his way."

"You left him behind?" Skeele asked.

"No. We were simply faster than him." Shay moved toward the door.

"How much faster?" Skeele asked.

But Shay had gone inside and the only one to greet Skeele's gaze was Nero, who was smirking and huffed with pride.

———

Teari never panicked when she saw the blood and the knife. She took one look at Jed and began healing him. She removed the knife and cast it aside saying, "at least there was no poison in this blade." She stitched Jed's back then went to work on the hundreds of tiny bites on his arms and legs from the spiders and roaches and beetles and Demons.

Shay's hand never left Jed, she stroked his dirty and disheveled hair and whispered in his ear to *hold on* and *come back* and *stay*. At least he was still breathing, although shallow and slow. She wanted to kiss him, wanted to see the color of his eyes and pink flush his cheeks with life; she'd waited so long. She'd been too long without him and this was torture.

Chel was waiting in the corner of the room, trying not to be disruptive to Teari. He'd cleaned his wounds and bandaged them the best he could all the while muttering about how Meg needed her own healer and needed to stop borrowing her father's.

After some time, Chel pulled Shay from Jed's side and began washing and bandaging her wounds. He found the bitemarks from Krelp, and the bruises on her inner elbows from where Alastor had drained her.

"Will you be okay?" Chel asked Shay, holding her arms out straight, his voice low, his eyes focused on the bites. "Did he hurt you in other ways?" Chel paused before clarifying, "Do you need to be alone with the healer?"

Shay shook her head. "I'm fine. I just want him to wake." She glanced at Jed as Teari was covering him with a sheet, tucking it around his shoulders.

Teari washed her hands at the sink before approaching Chel and Shay.

"He just needs rest," Teari said. "He'll be fine. But you, there's something we need to take a look at."

Shay went still, afraid that Chel had told Teari about her transforming with Nero during the fight in the dungeon of the black mansion. She didn't want Teari to know. After all, Shay was simply a human who shouldn't be able to do things like that.

"You have a new wound," Teari was pointing to Shay's hip.

Shay had barely noticed that the dress was not much more than shreds. Krelp had cut it up and now it hung off her body in strips and threads, threatening to fall the rest of the way apart.

"Go get her some clothing," Teari told Chel.

He nodded and left he infirmary.

Teari motioned to the cot next to Jed's. "Sit. Show me."

Shay climbed onto the cot and leaned to the side, showing Teari the brand on her hip. "Alastor did it.

The... the Demon who took me. He said that I would always return to him. It's never healed."

"Does it hurt?" Teari asked, examining the mark, probing Shay's tender skin but never touching the rune directly.

"It hurts less than it used to." Shay looked away, focused on anything in the room besides the ugly mark on her hip.

"It smells rotten. I think it's infected." Teari's hand hovered over the red edges and burned black skin. "The rune, I've never seen it before."

Teari pulled a curtain around them. "Remove that torn dress," she said, handing Shay a white gown from the bedside table. "Let me get a few things while you change."

Shay removed the strips of dress and found more bite marks from Krelp. Her hands shook as she realized how much worse the situation could have been. Even though Alastor was a bastard he'd come in the room when Shay started screaming. He was the one to stop Krelp from feasting on her whole body. It was the last redeeming moment the Demon had before he died. Shay shivered as she draped the gown over herself and lay back on the cot.

Teari returned with a tray of cloths and tins. She set the tray down and sat on the edge of the bed. "This is probably going to hurt," she warned.

Shay nodded. Nothing had hurt as much as Alastor telling her Jed was dead. Shay was certain she could take anything now. Teari could cut off her leg and Shay was certain she'd barely feel it.

Teari set a warm cloth on the brand for a few moments, then dabbed it dry. She held her hands over the mark, trying to heal it, but nothing happened.

"Just as I feared," Teari said. "My healing magic won't work on this Demon-made thing. We'll have to stick with poultices and clean dressings."

Teari layered the brand with a thick coat of minty smelling salve. She wrapped Shay's hip in a clean bandage then began inspecting her other wounds. Chel had done a decent job cleaning them. Teari's eyes kept falling on the scar on her thigh.

"Leave it alone," Shay finally said. "It's part of me now."

Teari frowned. "I wish I could have helped you with that."

"It doesn't matter anymore."

Teari cleaned up and opened the curtain. "I'm headed back to Gabriel's realm. I can come back in a few days."

"And Jed?" Shay asked.

"He'll wake up when he's ready." Teari paused and it seemed like she wanted to say more but she didn't.

Teari left and Shay heard voices outside the infirmary doors.

Shay slipped off the cot and padded over to Jed. She pulled back his sheet and crawled into bed next to him. Her fingers traced the scars on his chest, old and new.

"Stay," she whispered in his ear and kissed his jaw.

Jed twitched. His arm tightened around her. His voice sounded like nothing more than a breath but Shay heard Jed loud and clear. "*Stunning.*"

She smiled as she tucked herself against Jed, her head nestled on his shoulder. And she promised herself, maybe this time she wouldn't go outside alone in the dark. This time she might listen and if she listened, she prayed Jed would too.

FORTY-SIX

Jed was somewhere dark and warm. He didn't remember the knife going in his back, he only recalled the sickening feeling of dropping at Shay's feet before he could kiss her and let her know she was everything to him. He missed Shay terribly; her smell, her softness... everything. Jed had just gotten her back and she was gone again, slipped through his fingertips. He had to find her.

Jed wasn't exactly sure where he was. There was fog, the familiar train station that he and his mother used to travel the Northeast. He stood near a wooden bench, waiting, unsure if he was waiting for the train or something else. He scrutinized the sky, the tracks, the steps behind him. There was nothing, until there was a familiar voice.

"Baby," Clara said, "where have you been all this time?"

Jed's chest filled with emotion. Last time he'd seen his mother, he was floating in the ocean ready to give up on life.

"What are you doing here?" she asked again.

"I got hurt," he motioned to his back, "during a fight with a Demon."

"Let me look." Her voice was soft and concerned. He felt her touch on his shoulders.

"It appears you've been stabbed," Clara was stepping around him, her hand never leaving him. "Must've been a sly creature to get past you."

Jed nodded. "It was." Emotion swelled. "Am I dead?"

Clara shook her head. "No, baby, you're somewhere in between." She searched his face. "You're not supposed to be here but let's not waste this time together. What troubles you?"

His mother always had the answer to everything, when he was a child and then again when he'd see her in dreams or near death experiences.

He paused for too long, couldn't find the words to explain what he'd been going through.

Clara smiled, somehow she knew. "Did you meet a nice girl?"

Jed's chin trembled and the noise that came out of his throat sounded like a cry and a laugh. He covered his face, realizing he'd lost her in death. Unexpectedly, ironically, he'd been the one to die in the end.

Warm hands pulled at his wrists. "Baby, tell me about her. Is she pretty? Strong? Tell me everything."

Jed looked up to Clara's warm smile. He wiped his face. "She's beautiful. Long blue hair."

"Blue?" Clara smiled wide. "To match your aura?" Her hands outlined the glowing blue aura that surrounded him. "Have you protected her?"

Jed was silent for a moment as he chose his words. "She protected me. Once she killed an Angel that had the upper hand. She dragged me to safety. She saved me."

"I knew she'd be strong."

"But she's so small. So... human." Jed didn't like saying the phrase like a flaw but he didn't know another way.

"I was small compared to you as a man." Clara motioned to his height. "Much smaller than you are now and I did just fine." Clara took his hands and dragged him to the bench, forcing him to sit. "Tell me more."

"She is a bit defiant. She's gotten hurt."

Clara waved the concern away. "Think back to all we lived through and how many times you helped bandage me up. It's not uncommon for humans to get hurt. The scars show we *lived*. That's all anyone wants, to live. What's her name?"

"Shay." Jed squeezed Clara's hands. "I wish you were alive to meet her."

"She sounds lovely. And you seem hesitant about something."

"We saved her from a Demon... again."

"*We*? You're making friends? Wonderful. I always wanted you to have friends but it was too dangerous. Keep going." Clara smiled, eager to hear more.

"I'm afraid that she'll get hurt again and again. I just want to keep her safe. I think the best way to keep her safe is to keep my distance."

Clara was shaking her head. "Baby, enjoy the time you get with Shay and stop keeping her at arm's length. I didn't keep you alive all those years so you could live half a life."

Jed nodded, solemn, understanding.

The blare of a train horn interrupted them. Clara stood. "It's my time to go."

Jed stood and she hugged him tightly, not wanting to let go. Clara rose up on her toes and kissed his cheek.

"Baby, I love you. You're going to wake up soon. Go *live*."

Jed was beaming as Clara stepped onto the empty

train. The doors closed and it pulled away from the station.

—————

Now

Jed opened his eyes. Shay was there, asleep, her leg thrown over his and her chin tucked against his chest. He took a deep breath, inhaling the scent of her. His body ached but he'd never felt better than with Shay next to him. She made a soft sound in her sleep.

Jed twisted his body to face her, felt the stitches in his back pulling. He touched her face, tucked the strands of blue behind her ear. His fingertips traced her neck, paused on the scars from where the Demon had fed. He pulled the sheet back and found more on her arms. He moved the thin gown she was wearing and saw marks on her legs. If the Demon bastard wasn't already dead, he'd kill the beast over and over again for marking her skin.

Shay's eyes flashed open. "You're awake," she murmured.

Jed kissed her, gently, savoring the softness of Shay's lips and her taste. Her body pressed against his and her small hands roamed over his shoulders and chest and back.

"Does it hurt?" she asked, her fingertips moving over the bandage on his back.

"Not even close to how much it hurt nearly losing you." He leaned back, searching her eyes. "Did they hurt you? I don't want to scare you or hurt you more."

"Teari said the bite marks would go away eventually." She gazed into his eyes, feeling warm all over. "You won't hurt me." She slid her leg over his, up his hip, and pulled him closer. "I don't want to hurt you."

Jed smiled. "Never." He was toying with the knot at the closure of her gown before he tugged it loose. "I want you like never before."

Shay's hands slid into his hair and tugged him closer for a kiss. Jed's hand slid the gown aside and their mouths opened, tongues tangled in a kiss that had been too long in the waiting.

Jed's free hand roamed her body, cupped her breasts, his thumb pressing over her pebbled nipple. Shay moaned and threw her head back. Jed kissed down her neck, sucking and licking along her clavicle, her chest, until he reached her breast with his mouth. He sucked as his hand roved over her hip, squeezed her backside before deft fingers trailed to her front and down to the vee of her thighs.

Jed shifted to brace himself above her and tugged Shay's body under his. She squealed, pressed her breasts upward for him to suck and kiss. He paused and she whined with the loss of his warm mouth on her body.

"It's not too much is it? Too fast?" Jed's fingers were pressed against her core.

"Never," Shay whispered before glancing at the door. "Someone might come in."

Jed whispered a spell that sounded like satin sheets dragging against each other, and the door locked. "No one will enter," he promised.

Shay kissed him again, pressing herself upwards so his fingers slid further between her legs. "Please," she begged. "Please, don't stop."

Jed's forehead dropped against hers as he pushed his fingers inside, stretching her, readying her.

Shay's hips moved to the same motion. Her hands gripped his hair, pulling him in for a deep kiss. He felt good, too good. He always did. She felt his length and hardness against her thigh. Shay reached down and took him in her hand, stroking.

"Fuck," Jed moaned, breaking their kiss. "I never want to stop."

"Don't stop." Shay moved her leg, making space for him. Jed's fingers left her. He shifted and Shay felt his thickness begin to stretch her.

They moved together slowly, so slow Shay thought she might die from the pleasure of it. Jed kissed her everywhere; lips, skin, breasts. Shay moaned softly when Jed ground his hips against hers. He held her close, one hand under her hips and one behind her back, crushing her to him, never letting go.

Tears stung Shay's eyes as her arms tightened around him. "Never let me go," she whispered. "Please."

"Heaven and Hell will have to fight me for you. I'll never let go. You're mine. Forever," Jed promised with a searing kiss that tore at her soul. Jed's hips jerked and tension swelled inside Shay. They rode into oblivion together.

FORTY-SEVEN

Sparrow stood outside the door of a burning mansion. The air was filled with smoke and ash, smelled like fresh cinders. He sent shadows under the door to smother the smoke and flame before kicking the door open.

He searched the burning ruins, held the walls and ceiling up with shadows until he was able to find what he was looking for.

Alastor was half burned with a knife in his heart. If the Raven King had been any later, the Demon would be dead. Sparrow's shadows smothered the flames on Alastor's clothing and skin. He reached down and pulled the knife out of Alastor's chest, tucked it into his leathers and waited.

Alastor's eyes fluttered open and the wound slowly closed. He stared up at Sparrow.

"What have you done?" Alastor asked.

"Saved your life." Sparrow paced, ash and ichor collecting on the feathers of his wings that dragged on the floor. "I suggest getting to your feet so we can leave this place before it collapses." Sparrow was inspecting Krelp's charred remains.

"Where is Shay?" Alastor asked.

"Not here." Sparrow waited for the Demon to move.

"I will burn all of Hellscape until I find her. Is that what you want, Raven King?"

"I will drain you to a husk." Sparrow threatened.

"Try," Alastor challenged.

"Get fucked," Sparrow said.

"I'd like to but you kidnapped my girl."

"She is not your girl. Erase her memory from your mind." Sparrow crossed his arms, gripping the basilisk blade in his right hand.

Alastor tipped his head. "Whose girl is she then?" He leaned forward, his brow wrinkled as he searched Sparrow's face for an answer. "If she's not my girl, whose girl is she?"

"The Nephilim. Leave them alone. You are mine now."

Alastor's eyes went wide as he read between the lines.

Then he threw his head back and laughed out loud like a coyote at midnight who'd found fresh meat. "You? You! Fucking sick. Just like your father. The apple doesn't fall far from the tree. I have to say, Raven King, I didn't expect this from you but I'm not surprised in the least bit." He sat, crossed his leg over his knee and asked, "What do you want? How many?"

"As many as I can get."

"Nah." Alastor shook his head. "That's not how this works."

Sparrow palmed the basilisk tooth knife. "I could impale you with this again and you can continue on in stasis with nothing. I pulled this from your blackened heart. You owe me a life debt. I don't need to make a deal. *You do!*"

Sparrow slammed the tip of the basilisk blade into the wooden table. "Eighty percent."

Alastor shook his head. "Nah. I can't run this on twenty percent. I need the funds. Thirty percent."

"Sixty."

The Demon and the Raven King went back and forth with numbers and values until Sparrow began to get annoyed.

"Your father only wanted five percent," Alastor revealed.

"I am not my father."

"Remiel was a greedy bastard. Heard that Queen Meg drained him dry." Alastor prodded.

"I'm not here to talk about *your* Queen." Sparrow's features went blank.

Alastor chuckled. He'd heard rumors about the fated Meg and Sparrow and their epic downfall. Seems the Raven King was still butthurt over it all.

"I killed her once already. I'd do it again. She is nothing." Sparrow picked up the basilisk tooth knife. "I'll kill you in a heartbeat if you don't remain on topic." Shadows pooled around his feet with the threat.

Alastor was rubbing his temples, wishing he'd taken Shay like he'd wanted to all those weeks. Now it was too late. He'd never taste her like he desired. This was a game he was quickly losing.

"Fifty fifty," Alastor finally said.

"Deal." Sparrow led the Demon out of the crumbling mansion, stopping once they were outside its doors and the whispers of Hellnight greeted them.

"Now." Sparrow stepped closer. "Recall the rune you branded into Shay."

Alastor's eyes lit with fire.

"You think I'd forget? Remove it."

"I need her here." Alastor licked his lips.

"Fuck that. Remove it remotely." Sparrow spun the basilisk blade between his fingers with the intent of smashing it into Alastor's skull if he didn't comply. He'd hate to lose all those souls but Shay was worth more. Combined, Sparrow would be the most powerful King in the Seven Kingdoms of Heaven. More powerful than Gabriel, Meg's father, more powerful than Babylon or the Deacons.

A sudden tick quirked Sparrow's cheek and he thought he heard the call of a barn owl in the night. He ignored it.

Alastor glared, then stood tall, adjusting his burnt suit, and rubbing a hand over his newly scarred face. He needed a healer; he couldn't be walking around looking like a melting marshmallow. He had skin to trade and a partner to keep happy. Alastor grinned inwardly; things were looking up with a King from the Seven Kingdoms of Heaven on his side.

No, he wouldn't fix his face, Alastor finally decided. He'd leave the scars as a reminder to what distraction brings.

FORTY-EIGHT

"SOMETHING BAD IS COMING to this place," Teari warned Meg and Skeele.

"How do you know?" Meg asked. "Plenty of bad omens have been delivered to me. They've never been right, completely. This is Hell, bad shit happens."

Teari clasped her hands and focused on Meg. "You all need to be on high alert."

"Just fucking tell me what the deal is, Teari," Meg said.

"I can't say." Teari's face was impassive.

"Bullshit." Meg was fidgeting. "Tell me or get the fuck out."

Teari's brows rose. "Are you serious?"

"I'll cast you out of my realm–"

Teari's face twisted. "I'll file this under you're probably hangry." She glanced to Skeele. "Feed her will you?"

And then Teari was gone, having stepped through the portal and gone back to Gabriel's realm in Heaven.

Skeele turned to Meg, "Was that necessary?"

Meg sighed and ran hands through her hair. "She'll forgive me, she always does."

Skeele stared.

"Fine. Fine! I'll send her a letter or something apologizing."

"Hell is a large realm," Skeele reminded Meg. "Intel is important no matter who it comes from."

"What have the Hellions reported?" Meg asked.

"The problems are relatively mild compared to what went on here during Lucifer's reign." Skeele was looking away from Meg.

"Tell me the truth." Meg's eyes narrowed on him.

Skeele led her away. "Not here."

FORTY-NINE

Meg purchased the Peabody Library after speaking with Jed and deciding on a place where Jed and Shay could hide. There was too much risk in Hell for them to stay.

Meg was rich on the Earthen plane. Her mother had left her a boatload of money and since she didn't spend much time there, purchasing a foreclosed library was the perfect expenditure. The structure had good bones, the walls solid, good plumbing, and power. It was pre-warded from the time Declan lived there. Iron-strong wards guarded every entrance, heck even the sidewalk had wards carved underneath the cement.

Peabody Library was a sanctuary now. It would remain boarded and warded so Jed and Shay could live in safety and seclusion. And Nero. There was plenty of room for Nero.

———

"Stay out of trouble," Chel warned, hugging Shay goodbye.

"If I find trouble, you'll be the first Hellion I call," Shay promised.

Chel turned to Jed, slapping him on the back. "You're still a piece of shit." Jed's eyes widened as Chel grabbed a handful of shirt and yanked him closer, hugging him like an old friend. "But I guess you'll do. Take care of her."

"I always will," Jed promised, a chill passing through him when Chel stepped away.

"See ya around, clotpole." Chel waved before walking back to his post near the castle gates.

"I'm not comfortable with you *poofing* these two back and forth between Hell and the Earthen plane," Skeele grumbled as he crossed his arms.

Nero whinnied expectantly.

"No," Meg warned the stallion. "You can cross the Veil on your own. Meet us at the library."

Nero huffed and stomped the dirt at Meg's audacity. He didn't want Shay out of his sight on the Earthen plane, but he knew how to get there, *fast*. Nero grinned, tipped his head down and readied himself, eager to beat Meg at her own game of traveling faster than the speed of light.

"You want to come too?" Meg held out her hand and wiggled her fingers in Skeele's direction. "Freshly fed means I'm *uber* powerful right now. Come on."

"Fine." Skeele stomped closer, grumbling in Hellspeak. He lowered his voice and murmured something to Meg, calling her *Night Owl* as he kissed her neck and whispered dark promises in her ear, making Meg close her eyes and moan like she'd eaten chocolate cake.

"Dare ya," Meg said as she stared him down. "I'll even call you Kal." She winked. "We can get shrimp in the panhandle."

Recognition sparked as Shay took Meg's hand, ready to travel in her swift and violent manner of *poofing* from place to place.

"Okay," Meg smirked at the three. "Don't let go, this is gonna be fast." She closed her eyes and... *poof!*

Shay wobbled, feeling dizzy and nauseous. She leaned against Meg, knowing Meg didn't like to be touched. Something must've changed in the queen because instead of pulling away, Meg gripped Shay to steady her.

Shay's fingers grabbed two feathers and just before

she pulled them out, her knee bent and she dropped to the ground. Meg went with her and never felt the sting of feathers being pulled out of her wing.

"I'm sorry," Shay said with a flustered giggle, gripping her scarred thigh. "It's this leg, didn't heal right. I think the travel between realms hit me too hard." She looked up at Meg. "Are you okay?"

"I'm fine." Meg smiled but her eyes narrowed on Shay. Meg let go. "I can't lift you." She touched her swollen belly then motioned to Skeele.

Shay realized it was hard for Meg to admit she couldn't do something. Shay had that same problem sometimes.

The Hellion lifted Shay to her feet like she weighed nothing. Jed was there to take Shay into his arms and steady her; he didn't see when Shay tucked the feathers of the Night Owl into her pocket.

No one did.

FIFTY

A HORSE IN A LIBRARY... it sounded ridiculous but Nero didn't give two shits about what people would think. He liked the sound his hooves made on the wooden floor, liked the sound on tile even better. Jed had built him a real bed in one of the rooms near where he and Shay slept. It was better than matted straw or fresh grass. Horses didn't typically sleep on mattresses or have a private room with four walls and a bathroom. But Nero did. The tub was filled with fresh water every night. Nero took to the change as though he'd always lived inside like a human.

Nero never trotted fast in the library, he took his time, he went *slow*. The hallways were wide and the rooms large. When he was wandering between the stacks of books he was careful not to tip them over by rubbing his sides against them. He stayed in the middle and gazed at the rows of books that smelled like they just might be a tasty snack. A tunnel led to the river where Nero could stretch his legs and graze in the moonlight.

There were runes of protection drawn on the walls and the doorframes but they were far enough away that they didn't make Shay's skin itch and feel tight. What-ever she'd felt in the suite at the castle in the burning caves, she wasn't feeling it here.

Jed was relaxed, like the days at the graveyard chapel. The creases had left his face and he didn't seem so stuck in his own head. He was quick to talk and kiss and touch. He was quick to fall into bed without a second thought, touching Shay like she was all he'd ever wanted, like she was a goddess he worshipped.

They spent their days reading and lounging. They built a rooftop garden, shielded from the nearby city. Peabody library looked abandoned and was warded to appear so. Nobody would know from the outside looking in that a Demon horse, a Demon poison-stained girl, and a half-breed Angel sought refuge in the old library.

Jed and Shay and Nero lived in peace. No one knew where they were besides Meg and Skeele. Jed didn't care to leave the safety of the library any more than to walk by the river in the moonlight with Nero.

They spent their days reading, sleeping, and playing board games from before Shay was born. She got really good at cards and betting and hiding her reactions if she had a good hand or a shit hand.

Shay was leaning against Jed, both immersed in a book, enjoying the silence of the library and the warmth of each other's bodies. Suddenly, Shay's pupils went black and a shiver tore up her spine.

"What was that?" Jed asked, turning toward her.

"Nothing," Shay said.

Shay and Nero made eye contact. The horse was resting near the lit fireplace like a dog. A deal had snapped into place. The only one waiting for delivery was Sparrow's.

That fuck resurrected Alastor.

"Jed, baby?" Shay inched closer. "Have you ever thought about which one of the Archangels fathered you?"

"Yes."

"Do you know who it is? It might come in handy in the future." She tucked blue hair behind her ear and tried her best to look innocent.

Jed was searching her eyes. He was so tired of running and hiding and being back in Peabody library was the most peaceful he'd felt since the first time he'd lived here. He missed his friend Declan and many memories had flooded him walking through the familiar doors. The rooms where he'd learned to harness his magic seemed haunted now.

Jed stood and walked away. He explored the alphabetical markers on stacks until he came across a familiar book about Archangels.

Jed returned to the table where they'd been reading. Shay's bare legs were hanging over the arms of a wooden chair.

"My mother told me once. Only once." Jed was flipping the pages, smoothing his fingers over ages old script and parchment. His fingertips made a sweeping sound, like the dragging of Angel wing feathers. He stopped on the Archangel Michael. He tapped his finger on the page. "This one. She seemed afraid to say his name out loud but she was already dead so he couldn't do anything to her."

"She came to you as a ghost?" Shay asked.

Jed nodded, remembering the flooded boat and how he'd barely made it back to shore. He'd be at the bottom of the sea if she hadn't come to him. He wanted to tell Shay that Clara had come to him when he was unconscious, after Alastor had stabbed him but he would wait for another time to tell her that story.

Shay shifted in her seat, curling her legs underneath

her and leaning close. Blue hair fell on Jed's arm. "Your father is the Archangel Michael."

Shay's leg scar burned. Her stomach ached. She felt that familiar tug. "We're about to be pulled to the Crossroads," she warned Jed.

"Okay." He kissed her quickly. "Be safe." He searched her face, wanting to be there to protect her, afraid that she'd get hurt. He finally accepted that she'd never be completely safe and he'd relish whatever time he was allowed to have with her. "I want to come with you."

"I must go with Nero."

Jed nodded knowingly, accepting.

"Make us dinner?" Shay asked as the tugging in her stomach became more intense.

"What do you want?" Jed asked.

"French toast. Extra bacon. Hot coffee." Shay smiled before she was wrenched away to the Crossroads.

-The End-

Preview of Veil of Shadows Book 11 [Untitled and Unedited]

Note from the author: Veil of Shadows Books 11+ will jump to the future, one where there is a war, tragedy, enemies to lovers, second chance romance. It's time for Sparrow's redemption...

Reminder: this is a preview of an unedited work in progress, names may change, scenes may change, plotting may change during editing. Below is just a rough draft of the next book for your enjoyment. Make sure you're following my website/blog to get more chapter previews and announcements.

Chapter 1

Nightingale has found me in a dream. I want to tell her

she promised to stop. I'm sitting on a soggy dock, feet dangling in cool, dark water. I'm watching the loons floating in the morning mist. Nightingale is running toward me. Running on water, arms out, terrified look on her face. The loons scramble away, their wings flapping against the water as they soar low. I want to yell at Nightingale for ruining my fucking peace. But, this must be something serious because she hasn't come to me in a dream like this in years.

"What is it?" I ask.

"Wake up, Meg." She's shaking my shoulders. "Get up! Get up now! They're storming the castle. Wake up you must save your children!" she screams in my face.

My eyes flash open.

I sit up in bed, smell acrid creosote. It's familiar but too intense, too fresh. The window is open, no birds chirp, no owls hoot. There's fresh smoke, the hammering of stone, shouting.

Skeele shifts, moving closer. Someone howls, there's footsteps in the hallway.

"Wake up!" I yell to Skeele, launching myself out of bed.

He's on his feet, naked, ready to fight. A spec of dried blood on his lip. There's no slow morning stretches with our limbs rubbing together, savoring the memories and ache of last night.

"Clothes." I throw him a pair of pants and shirt.

"The babies." His eyes are wide, terrified. "Get them." Skeele's shirt gets caught on his horns, he tugs hard, tearing it in a rush.

He calls them babies still but they are much older, too old to be called babies, they're teenagers now but he's never stopped. I guess compared to him they will always appear to be babies. Young, innocent, his. Something he never thought he'd have. Bred to serve the throne, he took on so much more.

I grab clothes and throw them on. I get my bag, my blade, and weapons, they've been ready to go since Teari warned me of something terrible coming years ago. I threatened to kick her out of my realm for it because she didn't give me details, she just had a feeling, a premonition. She was right and I'm thankful she told me. Otherwise I wouldn't have a bugout bag packed and ready, and a plan.

"Here." Skeele tosses me the jar of Snowy Owl feathers from my bedside.

Poof. I leave the room.

"Children," I whisper shaking them awake. "Wake up right now."

Remington launches up straight with a deep intake of breath. Rue is quieter, green eyes flash open, her arms jerk to the sides, gripping the sheets. "Are we going to die?" she asks.

"Get moving." I throw her blankets back and don't answer her question. I can't answer her question because fear is more than a flood threatening to overtake my body, it's a tsunami, an earthquake, something thoroughly consuming that clogs my throat and traps my words.

This is not new. I have been attacked by evil before, but that was when my world was small. The stakes are higher than ever now. I couldn't protect the seed in my womb then, but now... now I could lose everything I didn't think I deserved. Fate has been cruel and unfair but I don't have time to dwell on it now.

Remington and Rue scramble out of bed, and when they smell the smoke that seeps under their door and hear the commotion echoing in the hall, they move quickly and meet me in their closet.

"Get clothes," I say. "Boots, knives, leather jackets and pants."

They listen. They listen because Teari warned me thirteen years ago that something was coming, something bad and every day since we've prepared.

Clea arrives, wisps of white swirl into her ethereal

form. "Let me say goodbye," Clea's voice breaks through before she's fully formed. "I must say goodbye to them."

My mother's lips are deep red, her transparent skin a ghastly white, but, she doesn't scare them. This is all they know of their grandmother. She died the day I was born so it is all I know of her as well.

"Hurry, Clea," I warn, collecting more clothing and tucking knives into Rue's pockets.

"Oh, children," her form turns solid, "be safe." She hugs them together, one on each arm, hugged so tight they might complain that they can't breathe but instead they hug her back just as fiercely.

"What have you seen?" I ask Clea, tossing a pack to Remington. He straps it on and pulls the clips tight.

"Demons from the mountains. Bugs and snakes and roaches." Clea shivers with disgust. "The dark force is strong, familiar."

"Did you see a face?" I ask, helping Rue tighten her pack.

"Not yet," Clea says. "I had to stop and say goodbye, I'll go back."

"Be careful," I warn.

"Hide them well," Clea says with a warm smile, patting each child on a cheek then pinching them. "I wish you could take my bones so I could go with you and have more time. Our women are cursed with losing children."

"They won't be lost," I say. "They'll be in hiding."

Clea nods and straightens her back. "Hurry." She turns toward the door. "Something is coming."

I nod. "Help the Hellions. Skeele is in charge while I'm gone."

I take Rue's hand then Remington's. *Poof*–we're gone.

CHAPTER 2

Alastor trekked from his hovel in the mountains to the black lakes of Hell's Adirondacks. He had one goal, to secure a Basilisk. He didn't have a castle to defend, yet, but he'd need the creature to get there.

Alastor drove to Old Forge, taking Interstate-81 but avoiding all of Pennsylvania. He passed herds of the walking dead, a smirk crossing his face as he counted them and calculated how large his army would become.

Alastor turned off the exit toward Interstate-481 north, then turned on Interstate-90 east. He passed farmland and dense forests. He saw signs for the Safe

House nearby. He made a mental note to have those taken down. They wouldn't be a factor much longer. Alastor merged onto 365 E and veered off onto Eastern Rock Rd. The Jeep jostled across the busted parking lot. He turned onto Moose River Road and drove past old houses and grocery stores. The Black River roared from nearby, the waters turbid and angry and the slick serpentine backs of the basilisk swim.

There were spawning.

He stood on a giant rock, planning his next move. There were plenty of ways to fish for a basilisk.

Alastor jumped down to lower rocks and made his way toward the shallow pool of baby basilisk.

A giant head rose from the surface of the river, watching. Rows of sharp teeth and a warning hiss.

"Come on ya slimy, bitch," Alastor said, pulling a knife from his belt.

He crouched, reaching into the pool of babies. The mother swam closer, teeth bared. Alastor reached into the water and grabbed a small one. The creature squealed ear-piercingly. Alastor cut it in half and tossed the body back into the water, turning it a murky red. The mother moved closer, jaws gnashing, threatening. It didn't scare Alastor, he had a plan. Alastor jumped in the dark water and made quick work of slaughtering the baby basilisk. Within minutes, he was saturated in bloody river water. Alastor rubbed the pieces of basilisk on his body, dipped his head and coated his hair and clothing in their blood. He bathed, rubbing their blood on his arms and neck.

The mother basilisk slithered closer, confused. Her children dead but Alastor smelling just like them. Being a creature of darkness, she followed the Demon who smelled like her children because if he smelled like her children, then he must be one, the only one, and she would protect him until the very end.

Alastor tucked pieces of bleeding basilisk into his pockets so the smell remained fresh. He emerged from the river, covered in blood and bits of flesh and bone. He walked back to his Jeep, smiling as the mother basilisk followed him. A menacing shadow at his back.

Chapter 3

Meg

Peabody Library is dark. I wish I could have sent warning that I'd be coming, when we arrive, it sets off every ward in the in the building. Hm. After all these years Jed would ward his home against me, after I bought it for him. Typical Jed. The horse shows up to investigate first.

A shallow whinny greets us.

"Nero," I say. "Come clear this rune." I motion to the circle that's trapping us.

Nero shakes his head in a firm response of "no."

The damn horse is trained not to trust me. Perfect. I can't blame Jed and Shay, I've gotten them in plenty of trouble over the years. The probably don't want any surprises.

"Then go get Shay," I say. "And hurry."

Before the giant black stallion gets himself turned around, footsteps echo down the hall.

"Meg?" Shay's voice shouts.

"Shhh," Jed shushes her.

"Come free us," I holler. "I don't have much time." I

do my best to hide the panic in my voice. I have to get out of here, return to Hell and defend the castle.

"What shit-fuckery did you bring us this time?" Jed asks, turning the corner around a bookshelf, he stops short when he sees the children behind me. His eyes blow wide, knowing. "What's happening?" He moves closer but doesn't clear the rune of chalk on the floor.

"The castle in the burning caves is under attack." I shift on my feet, eager to get out of the circle in the middle of the room. I feel too exposed like this. Trapped with my children.

"You mean *your* throne is under attack?" Shay clarifies.

I nod. I don't want to admit it. I never wanted the throne it was part of the price for killing my grandfather, Lucifer.

Jed takes a few quick steps forward and scuffs his boot over the chalk on the floor.

I take a deep breath, and step away, dragging the children with me. I go to Shay. She helped me many years ago with a search and rescue, then again when I was imprisoned with the Deacons, she impersonated me to keep the throne of Hell safe.

"Wait," I say. "One more thing." I drop my bag off

my shoulder, unzip it and pull out the jar of snowy owl feathers. "Put this somewhere safe."

Shay reaches for the jar. It's small, not much more than a jelly jar. Etched glass, a stainless steel lid. These are the remains of my dead daughter, Elise. I swallow hard, tamping down emotion afraid that this night might leave me with three jars of feathers and no children.

There. I have left everything that I care about in Peabody library. Everything I never thought I'd have, I've left in the hands of others. It's a terrible feeling, leaving trust with others. Something that took me a long time to adjust to.

Chapter

Shay took the jar of mottled white and brown feathers, blinked and she was immediately transported back to a memory from a Crossroads Demon deal.

The air crackled with an ominous energy as the figure approached the crossroads, their steps hesitant yet filled with a sense of desperate determination. They bore the weight of something heavy upon their shoulders, their gaze haunted by the specter of tragedy that loomed over their existence.

It was a Deacon.

Nero backed up.

Shay tensed.

Deacons were the gatekeepers of balance between the Seven Kingdoms of Heaven, the Earthen plane and Hell. Why did one summon Shay and Nero?

"What is it that you seek, Deacon?" Shay asked.

The Deacon hesitated, their gaze flickering with uncertainty before they spoke, voice tinged with a mixture of power and desperation.

"No one can know that I'm here," the Deacon said.

Shay nodded. "Is that your deal?"

"No." the Deacon folded his hands. "This deal will be a great burden for both of us."

The Deacon kept looking over his shoulder and to the desert beyond. He'd drawn them to a crossroads in the middle of nowhere. They could see for miles even with only moonlight.

"There is a great darkness coming," the Deacon warned.

"That sounds like a warning, not a deal. Why did you call me here?" Shay didn't want to return to Alastor but she didn't want her time wasted by this creature.

The Deacon paused and closed his eyes, finding calm

and choosing his words carefully. "The deal is, you must take the children to safety and tell no one where they are. You must hide them until Clea's prophecy comes to fruition."

"What children?"

The Deacon held up a finger. "They are not born yet. When the time comes, you will know. You must agree to this now, before it's too late."

"What are you wishing to give me?" Shay asked, knowing that what the Crossroads Demon would take was not negotiable and typically unknown.

"I will give my life. Sooner rather than later."

Shay blinked again before glancing at Nero. His ear twitched with recognition.

"They'll be safe her. We won't let anything happen to them," Shay said.

Meg nodded, and Shay noticed the slight quiver in her bottom lip. Meg wouldn't fall apart though, she never did, always kept her feelings in check unless it was anger. She wasn't afraid to let her anger out, but love, that was a feeling Meg kept under wraps and Shay could understand why. Meg had let her love escape once, she'd loved the Raven King and he nearly killed her. He ruined her, wrecked her, left others to clean up what was left of her broken heart and bleeding body. Meg was right to have trust issues. Last time she trusted someone heart and soul, she'd nearly died. Shay would never forget the moment Jed arrived covered in blood and panicking that they'd die in Hell with Meg gone.

Shay focused on the children standing behind Meg. They seemed despondent, didn't show a spec of fear. They'd never been to the Peabody library, never been to the Earthen plane as far as Shay knew. Shay and Jed had met them multiple times during holidays and Sunday dinners that Meg held. Shay and Jed attended, both having no other family and feeling compelled since Meg bought the library and let them live there. The children knew Jed and Shay and Nero, but that was about it.

Shay reached out to Rue first and hugged her. She gripped Remington's shoulder and gave him a little shake as a greeting and a promise.

"We'll take good care of them, for as long as you need," Shay promised.

Rue didn't say a word but Shay noticed the slight tremble of her bottom lip, exactly like her mother. She'd have to learn how to hide that better. The girl swiped at long dark hair that had fallen across her eyes.

Jed was there, taking Remington aside and whispering to him, no doubt warning him of the Earthen plane and what the boy could and could not do while he was here.

Shay shook Meg's shoulder, "If you've got to burn it all to the ground, then let it *burn*."

A chill passed through Meg as Shay's eyes flashed black. It was a side-effect of the Demon poison Shay had trapped in a scar. She was tethered to the Crossroads Demon Nero, her horse. As a result, Shay had the ability to transform into something wraithlike.

Shay tipped the jar to the side, watched the feathers drift, and realized that they looked very much like Meg's wings.

Meg nodded.

Shay hugged her, worried that Meg might fail. No. No Shay wouldn't let that thought out into the wild. Never wanted it to become true. Meg was the strongest person Shay had ever met. Shay squeezed Meg tight, easy not to pinch her wings.

"Burn it all, Meg," Shay whispered in her ear. "You are formidable."

Meg wiped her eyes, she wanted to tell the children goodbye again but she'd been here too long. She needed to go back.

Meg raised a hand, gaze meeting her children's as she waved goodbye to them. She'd never prayed but at that moment, she did, and she prayed that it wouldn't be the last time she ever saw them.

Poof – Meg returned to Hell.

About the Author

M. R. Pritchard, a captivating author, delves into the profound clash between good and evil, the mystical realms of gods and monsters, and the intricate transformations of ordinary people into beings of immense power. Her gripping narratives often unfold within the haunting backdrop of apocalyptic or post-apocalyptic landscapes, offering a unique blend of suspense and wonder.

M. R. Pritchard is a two-time Kindle Scout winning author, her short story "Glitch" has been featured in the 2017 winter edition of THE FIRST LINE literary journal. Her short story "Moon Lord" has been featured in Chronicle Worlds: Half Way Home (Part of the Future Chronicles) and will be time capsuled on the moon on the Lunar Codex in 2024.

Visit her website MRPritchard.com and Subscribe. You'll get subscriber only content, updates, special previews of new projects, and book deals.

Midsummer Night's Dream: A Game of Thrones

<u>Poetry/Short Stories</u>

Consequence of Gravity

www.ingramcontent.com/pod-product-compliance
Lightning Source LLC
Chambersburg PA
CBHW061632190726
48289CB00006B/1574